THE DETECTIVE
AND THE
SOMNAMBULIST.

Mrs. Drysdale and Mrs. Potter.

THE DETECTIVE

AND THE

SOMNAMBULIST.

By ALLAN PINKERTON

Black Squirrel Books® 🐿®
an imprint of The Kent State University Press
Kent, Ohio 44242   www.KentStateUniversityPress.com

This facsimile and edition was produced using a scan of a first-edition copy of *The Detective and the Somnambulist.* The original edition is part of the Borowitz Collection in the Kent State University Special Collections and Archives and is reproduced with permission.

BLACK SQUIRREL BOOKS® 🐿®
Frisky, industrious black squirrels are a familiar sight on the Kent State University campus and the inspiration for Black Squirrel Books®, a trade imprint of **The Kent State University Press.**
www.KentStateUniversityPress.com

Published by The Kent State University Press, Kent, Ohio 44242
All rights reserved
ISBN 978-1-60635-415-5
Manufactured in the United States of America

First published by W. B. Keen, Cooke & Co., Chicago, 1875.

Cataloging information for this title is available at the Library of Congress.

24 23 22 21 20   5 4 3 2 1

EXPLORING THE BOROWITZ COLLECTION

Cara Gilgenbach
Special Collections and Archives, Kent State University

———

The Borowitz Collection, from which the editions of the Pinkerton detective stories are taken, was officially gifted to Kent State University in 1989 by Albert and Helen Borowitz of Cleveland, Ohio. The collection includes primary and secondary sources on crime as well as works of literature based on true crime incidents.

Albert and Helen Borowitz, both scholars themselves, built a scholarly collection—one that affords more than sufficient breadth and depth to support any number of research inquiries. The Borowitz Collection reflects the multidisciplinary expertise of Albert Borowitz (a Harvard graduate with degrees in classics, Chinese regional studies, and law) and his late wife, Helen Osterman Borowitz (a Radcliffe graduate and art historian with literary interests). In addition to collecting, Albert Borowitz is himself a scholar of true crime, having published over a dozen books and many articles on the topic, most notably his masterwork, *Blood and Ink: An International Guide to Fact-Based Crime Literature.*

The Borowitz collection is an extensive one, documenting the history of crime, with primary emphasis on the United States, England, France, and Germany from ancient times to the present day. It includes groups of materials on specific criminal cases that have had notable impacts on art, literature, and social attitudes. This provides the researcher with a wealth of material on those cases and their cultural effects. The collection includes nearly 15,000 volumes of books and periodicals, complemented by archival and manuscript collections. Special areas of note include an excellent collection of Sherlock Holmes and other Arthur Conan Doyle early editions; nonfiction and fiction works related to Jack the Ripper; nineteenth- and twentieth-century British and American crime pamphlets and broadsides; a Wild West collection; crime-related photographs, playbills, postcards, and other ephemera; and artifacts, graphics, and memorabilia related to crime.

The Borowitz Collection includes numerous works of detective stories, both fiction and nonfiction, including books from the Pinkerton Detective Agency series, which embody the collection's central theme, namely how real-life elements of crime infiltrate creative works and works of the imagination. Although true crime is the primary focus of the Borowitz Collection, it also contains notable holdings in several other topics and genres, including a vast collection of sheet music spanning more than two centuries of popular musical taste and distinguished literary collections.

The collection provides rich sources to users as diverse as crime historians, film documentarians, museum curators, television and radio producers, antiquarian book dealers, novelists, and faculty and students of history, American studies, women's studies, and criminal justice, to name just a few. Kent State University is proud to steward this collection, and the present project to republish the Pinkerton detective stories is a further outgrowth of our desire to make these interesting and informative resources available to a wider audience.

THE DETECTIVE AND THE SOMNAMBULIST

CONTENTS.

———

PREFACE

IN presenting to the public my third volume of Detective Stories, I desire to again call attention to the fact that the stories herein contained, as in the case of their predecessors in the series, are literally true. The incidents in these cases have all actually occurred as related, and there are now living many witnesses to corroborate my statements.

Maroney, the expressman, is living in Georgia, having been released during the war. Mrs. Maroney is also alive. Any one desiring to convince himself of the absolute truthfulness of this narrative can do so by examining the court records in Montgomery, Ala., where Maroney was convicted.

The facts stated in the second volume are well known to many residents of Chicago. Young Bright was in the best society during his stay at the Clifton House, and many of his friends will remember him. His father is now largely interested in business in New York, Chicago, and St. Louis. The events connected with the abduction of " The Two Sisters," will be readily recalled by W. L. Church, Esq., of Chicago, and others. The story of " Alexander Gay," the Frenchman, will be found in

the criminal records of St. Louis, where he was sentenced
for forgery.

So with the stories in this volume. The characters in
"The Detective and the Somnambulist," will be easily
recognized by many readers in the South. As the family
of Drysdale are still living and holding a highly respecta-
ble place in society, the locality is not correctly given, and
fictitious names are used throughout.

By reason of the peculiar nature of the circumstances,
the facts narrated in "The Murderer and the Fortune-
Teller," are known only to a small circle, but they can
readily be substantiated. Captain Sumner was never
informed of the means employed to influence his sister,
and his first knowledge of them will be obtained in
reading this book; but he will remember his own visit to
"Lucille," and will undoubtedly see that the affair was
managed exactly as I have stated.

In reading these stories, the reader will probably come
to the conclusion that the detection of criminals is a very
simple matter, and that any one with a moderate amount
of intelligence could have done just as well. To a
certain extent this is true, but not wholly. The plan
once adopted, it is not difficult to put it in execution;
but experience, judgment and tact are required to form a
plan which will bring out the real facts connected with
the crime. This done, the capture of the criminal is only
a question of time.

Legitimate, honest detective business is yet in its
infancy, but the trade, as at present generally conducted,
approaches the dignity of an art—a black art, unfortu-
nately, the object being accurately to distinguish the per-

centage of plunder which will satisfy the criminals and the real owners, the remainder being divided among the so-called detectives.

In point of fact, these fellows are worse than the acknowledged criminals, since they rob under the guise of honest men, and run little or no risk, while the actual thieves take their lives in their hands. It may safely be said that the average detective would rather be in league with the criminals of this city than opposed to them, and the great majority *are* so leagued; and until such a state of affairs is broken up, the criminals who have money will surely escape punishment.

ALLAN PINKERTON.

September, 1875.

THE DETECTIVE

AND THE

SOMNAMBULIST.

CHAPTER I.

ABOUT nineteen years ago, I was enjoying a short relaxation from the usual press of business in Chicago. I had only one or two really important cases on hand, and I was therefore preparing to take a much needed rest. At this time, my business was not nearly so extensive as it has since become, nor was my Agency so well known as it now is; hence, I was somewhat surprised and gratified to receive a letter from Atkinson, Mississippi, asking me to go to that town at once, to investigate a great crime recently perpetrated there. I had intended to visit my former home in Dundee, for a week or ten days, but, on receiving this letter, I postponed my vacation indefinitely.

The letter was written by Mr. Thomas McGregor, cashier of the City Bank, of Atkinson, and my services were called for by all the officers of the bank. The cir-

cumstances of the case were, in brief, that the paying-
teller had been brutally murdered in the bank about three
or four months before, and over one hundred and thirty
thousand dollars had been stolen. Mr. McGregor said
that no expense should be spared to detect the criminals,
even though the money was not recovered; that would be
an important consideration, of course, but the first object
sought was the capture of the murderers of poor George
Gordon, the late paying-teller.

Having already arranged my business for a brief absence, I was all ready for the journey, and by the next
train, I was speeding southward, toward Atkinson.

I arrived there early in the morning, of one of the
most delightful days of early spring. I had exchanged
the brown fields and bare trees of the raw and frosty
North, for the balmy airs, blooming flowers, and waving
foliage of the sunny South. The contrast was most
agreeable to me in my then tired and overworked condition, and I felt that a few days in that climate would re-
store my strength more effectually than a stay of several
weeks in the changeable and inclement weather of northern
Illinois. For sanitary, as well as business reasons, therefore, I had no occasion to regret my Southern trip.

My assumed character was that of a cotton speculator,
and I was thus able to make many inquiries relative to
the town and its inhabitants, without exciting suspicion.
Of course, I should have considerable business at the
bank, and thus, I could have frequent conferences with
the bank officials, without betraying my real object in
visiting them. I sent a note to Mr. McGregor, on my
arrival, simply announcing myself under a fictitious name,

and I soon received a reply requesting me to come to the bank at eight o'clock that evening. I then spent the day in walking about the town and gathering a general idea of the surroundings of the place.

Atkinson was then a town of medium size, pleasantly situated near the northern boundary of the State. The surrounding country was well watered and wooded, consisting of alternate arable land and rolling hills. The inhabitants of the town were divided into two general classes : the shop-keepers, mechanics, and laborers, formed the bulk of the population; while the capitalists, planters and professional men were the most influential. Most of these latter owned country residences, or plantations outside of the town, though they kept up their town establishments also. A small water-course, called Rocky Creek, skirted one side of the place, and many of the most handsome houses, were situated on, or near this beautiful rivulet. The whole appearance of Atkinson, and the surrounding country, indicated a thrifty, well-to-do population.

Having roamed about to my satisfaction, I spent the latter part of the afternoon at the hotel, where I met a number of the professional men of the county. I found that the hotel was occupied by many of the best families during the winter and spring, and I soon formed the acquaintance of several of the gentlemen. They greeted me with characteristic Southern hospitality, and I was pleased to see that my *role* as a Scotch speculator was quite an easy one to play; at least, no one ever appeared to suspect my real object in visiting Atkinson.

At the appointed hour I went to the bank, and was met

outside by Mr. McGregor, to whom I had been introduced during the day. He took me in through the private entrance, and we were joined in a few minutes by Alexander Bannatine, president, and Peter A. Gordon, vice-president, of the bank. Mr. Bannatine was about fifty years of age, but he looked much older, owing to his continuous and exhausting labors as a lawyer, during the early part of his life. Having made a large fortune by successful practice and judicious investments, he had retired from the active pursuit of his profession, and had joined several old friends in the banking business. Mr. Gordon was, also, about fifty years old. He had become wealthy by inheritance, and had increased his fortune by twenty years of careful attention to business. He was unmarried, and George Gordon, the murdered bank-teller, had stood in the relation of a son to his uncle; hence, there was an additional reason for the capture and conviction of the murderers. The recovery of the large sum of money stolen, would, alone, have been an important consideration, but Mr. Gordon was willing to spend a very extravagant amount in the detection of the criminals, even though the money might never be discovered.

We seated ourselves at a table in the cashier's room, and I prepared to take notes of all the facts then known by the gentlemen present.

"Now, Mr. Bannatine," I said, "please tell me everything connected with the case, which may be of service to me."

"Well, Mr. Pinkerton, I have not been connected with the bank so long, or so closely as Mr. McGregor," said

Mr. Bannatine, "and perhaps he had better give a short sketch of young Gordon's connection with the bank first."

"George Gordon was taken into our employ about five years ago," said Mr. McGregor. "He had previously acted as our agent in one of the interior towns, and when he became of age he was offered the place of paying-teller. Since then his obliging disposition, courteous manners, and faithful performance of duty, have endeared him to all his associates, and have given him the confidence of all persons with whom he came in contact. His character was spotless, and his devotion to duty was superior to all allurements ; he would never sacrifice one moment to pleasure which should have been given to business."

"Had he any associates among the fast men and women of the place ?" I asked.

"No, sir, not one," was the prompt reply ; "we have not been able to learn that he had any acquaintances even, among that class."

"Well, please proceed to state all the circumstances connected with the murder," I suggested.

"I was not at home at the time," said Mr. McGregor, "but I can give you many facts, and Mr. Gordon can add thereto. George was in the habit of remaining in the bank after office hours for the purpose of writing up his books, as he acted as book-keeper also. During the very busy seasons, he would sometimes be kept at work until long after dark, though this was unusual. Occasionally customers would come to the bank after the regular hours, and George would accommodate them, or I would do so, when I was present. We were both very careful about admitting outsiders after the bank had closed, and we never allowed any one to enter except well-known business men and old customers of the bank. We had large sums on hand at times, and George frequently said that we could not exercise too much care in managing our business. I mention this to show that he was not careless in his habits, but that, on the contrary, he always took the greatest precautions against fraud or violence."

"Were there any customers who were in the habit of coming in late?" I asked.

"Yes, there were several," replied Mr. McGregor; "for instance, Mr. Flanders, the jeweler, used to bring over his more valuable jewelry every afternoon to put into our vault; he would put it into a small box and leave it here about five o'clock. Then, our county clerk, Mr. Drysdale, used to stop frequently to make deposits in cases where other parties had paid money to him after banking hours. He was very intimate with George, and he used to stop to see him sometimes and walk out with him after his work was finished. Walter Patterson, also, was one of George's particular friends, and he has often stayed with George until nine or ten o'clock in the evening. Besides these there were several of our leading planters who would come in as late as eight o'clock to deposit funds, or to obtain cash for use early the next day."

"Did young Gordon have the keys to the vault?" I asked.

"Oh! yes," replied Mr. McGregor; "I was often called away on business for several days, and he used to act as cashier in my absence. He was in the habit of carrying the keys with him at all times; but his uncle advised him not to do so, as they might be taken from him by a gang of desperate characters, and the bank robbed. He had, therefore, given up the practice of taking the keys home with him after night-fall. Just about the time of the murder, we had one of the busiest seasons ever known; the cotton crop had been enormous, and sales had been very rapid, so that our deposits were unusually large. One morning I found that I must go to Greenville for several days, on business of great importance. Before going, I gave George full instructions upon all matters which might need attention during my absence; yet I felt, while on my way to the depot, that there was something which I had forgotten. I could not define what it was, but I hurried back to ask whether he could think of any thing further upon which he might wish my advice. I found him chatting with his friend, Mr. Drysdale. Calling him to one side, I said:

"'George, is there anything more upon which I can advise you?'

"'No, I guess not,' he replied; 'you will be back so soon that if there should anything new turn up, it can wait until you return.'

"'Well, be very careful,' I continued, 'and don't allow any one to come in here after dark. It may be an unnecessary precaution, but I should feel easier if I knew no one was admitted to the bank during my absence.'

"'Very well,' he replied, 'I shall allow only one or two of my personal friends to come in. There will be no harm in admitting them, for they will be an additional protection in case of any attempt on the bank.'

"I could offer no objection, and so we parted. I was gone about a week, when, having settled my business in

Greenville, I returned here. The first news I received was, that George Gordon had been found murdered in the bank that morning, the crime having been committed the night before. I will now let Mr. Peter Gordon, George's uncle, tell the circumstances, so far as he knows them."

Mr. McGregor was a careful, methodical man, about sixty years of age. He always spoke directly to the point, and in his story, he had evidently made no attempt to draw conclusions, or to bias my judgment in any way. Nevertheless, he showed that he was really affected by young Gordon's murder, and I saw that I should get more really valuable assistance from him, than from both of the other two. Mr. Gordon was greatly excited, and he could hardly speak at times, as he thought of his murdered nephew. His story was told slowly and painfully, as if the details were almost too much for him. Still, he felt that nothing ought to be neglected which would assist me, and so he nerved himsel to tell every little incident of the dreadful crime.

"I remember the day of the murder very distinctly, Mr. Pinkerton," he said. "Mr. Bannatine was obliged to visit his plantation that morning, and Mr. McGregor being away, as he has already told you, I spent most of the day at the bank with George. He was perfectly competent to manage all the business himself, Mr. Pinkerton for he was a very smart and trustworthy young man, the very image of my dear brother, who was drowned twenty years ago, leaving me to bring up George like my own son; but, as I was saying, I kept George company in the bank that day, more as a measure of safety, than because he needed me. Well we received a large amount of money that day in bank notes and specie, and I helped George put the money into the vault. When the bank closed, George said that he should work until five o'clock and then go home to dinner. I was anxious to go to my store, as business had been very heavy that day, and I had had no opportunity to attend to my own affairs; I therefore left the bank at four o'clock. George and I boarded at the hotel, and at dinner time, he came late, so that I finished before he did. About seven o'clock, George came down to the store, where I had gone after dinner. He sat a little while and smoked a cigar with me, and then said that he must return to the bank, as he had a great deal of work to finish up on the books; he told me, also, not to sit up for him, as it might be quite late before he came home."

"Were there any other persons present when he said this, Mr. Gordon?" I asked.

"Yes; there was a shoemaker, named Stolz, whom George had just paid for a pair of boots. Mr. Flanders, the jeweler, was there also, and he had his box of jewelry for George to lock up in the safe. There had been so many customers in his store that afternoon that he had not been able to take the box over before. There were several other persons present, I recollect now that you ask me about it, but I had not thought of the matter before, and I cannot recall their names."

"Well, I guess we can find out," I replied; "please go on. By the way, one question: had George drank anything at all during the day?"

"No, sir, nothing whatever. George used to smoke a great deal, but he *never* drank at a bar in his life; all his

2

young friends will tell you the same. He sometimes drank wine at meals at his own or a friend's table, but he never drank at any other place. He left my store about half-past seven o'clock, and Flanders went with him to leave his jewelry. Flanders' store is near mine, and he soon came back and chatted with me a short time. He has since told me that he did not enter the bank, but that he simply handed the case of jewelry to George on the steps of the private entrance, and George said to him: 'I won't ask you to come in, Flanders, for I have too much work to attend to, and I can't entertain you.' These are the last words that George is known to have spoken."

Here Mr. Gordon's agitation was so great that he could not speak for several minutes, but at length, he continued:

"I went to bed about ten o'clock that evening, and came down late to breakfast next morning. I did not see George anywhere around the hotel, but I thought nothing of that, as I supposed that he had gone to the bank. After breakfast, I got shaved, smoked a cigar, and then went to my store. In a few minutes, a man named Rollo, who has an account at the bank, came in and said:

"'Mr. Gordon, what is the matter at the bank this morning? It is now after ten o'clock, and everything is still shut up.'

"'What!' I exclaimed, 'the bank not opened yet! My nephew must be sick, though he was quite well yesterday evening. I will go to the bank with you at once, Mr. Rollo.'

"One of my clerks accompanied us, and on arriving at the bank, we found a cabinet-maker named Breed, trying to get in. I went and pounded on the front door several

"At this instant I flung open one of the shutters, and simultaneously I heard a cry of horror from my clerk."

times, but no one came. I then went to the private entrance and gave the signal by rapping, to let those inside know that one of the bank officers was at the door. We had a private signal known only to the officers, so that I was sure there must be something wrong when I found it unanswered. I had a dreadful feeling in my heart that something horrible had happened, and I was about to hurry away to the hotel, to see if George was there, when I casually let my hand fall upon the knob and turned it; to my surprise, the door yielded.

"By this time, quite a crowd had gathered outside, attracted by the unusual spectacle of the closed bank, and the knocking at the doors. I therefore left Mr. Rollo and Mr. Breed to keep the crowd from entering the side entrance, while my clerk and I threw open the heavy shutters of this room where we are now sitting. We then entered the main bank through yonder door, and while I went to open the outside blinds, which excluded every particle of light, my clerk walked down behind the bank counter. He suddenly stumbled over something and fell, and as he got up, he said that the floor was wet. At this instant, I flung open one of the shutters, and simultaneously I heard a cry of horror from my clerk. Running to the counter, I looked over and saw a terrible sight. My poor boy—"

Again Mr Gordon's feelings overcame him, and it was some time before he could go on. Finally he was able to resume his story, though he was frequently obliged to pause to wipe away his tears.

"My nephew's body was lying midway between his desk and the vault door; he had evidently been standing at his desk when he was struck, as was shown by the direction in which the blood had spirted. He had been murdered by three blows on the back of the head, the instrument used being a heavy canceling hammer, which we found close by, clotted with blood and hair. The first blow had been dealt just back of the left ear while George was standing at his desk; he had then staggered backward two or three steps before falling, and the second and third blows had been struck as he lay on the floor. Although it was evident that the first blow alone was sufficient to cause death, the murderer had been anxious to complete his work beyond any possibility of failure.

"The scene was most ghastly; George's body lay in a pool of blood, while the desks, chairs, table and wall, were spattered with large drops which had spirted out as the blows were struck. I shall never forget that terrible morning, and sometimes I awake with a horrible choking sensation, and think that I have just renewed the sickening experience of that day.

"Well, I immediately suspected that the murder had been committed to enable the murderer to rob the bank. I knew that George had no enemies who would seek his life, and there could be no other object in killing him inside the bank. The outer door of the vault stood slightly ajar, and as soon as I had satisfied myself that my nephew was dead—as indeed was evident, the body being quite cold—I sent my clerk to call Mr. Rollo and Mr. Breed into the bank, while he remained at the door. I told him to send any person whom he might see outside for the sheriff and the coroner. As I was saying, the vault door stood slightly open, and when the other gentlemen joined me I called their attention to the position of everything before I entered the vault. I found the keys in the lock of the inner door, and on opening the latter we saw that everything inside was in great confusion. Without making any examination, I closed and locked both doors, and sealed the key-holes with tape and sealing-wax. I determined to leave everything just as it was until the inquest should be held. The sheriff and coroner soon arrived, and a jury was impaneled immediately, as, by that time, the news had spread all over town, and the bank was surrounded by nearly all the best men in the place. In summoning the jury, the coroner put down for foreman the name of Mr. Drysdale, George's most intimate friend, but it was found that he was not in the crowd outside, and when they sent for him he begged so hard to be excused that he was let off.

"The inquest was held in this room, but nothing was moved from the bank except the body and the canceling hammer. The jury elicited nothing more than what I have told you, and they therefore adjourned to await the examination of our vault when Mr. McGregor and Mr. Bannatine returned, in the hope that some clue might be found therein. I forgot to mention that we found in George's hand a bill of the Planters' Bank of Georgia, of the denomination of one hundred dollars. It was clutched tightly, and he had fallen on that side, so that the murderer had not noticed it. Here it is, partly stained with blood," and Mr. Gordon handed me a bank note. He then continued:

"A messenger had been dispatched to inform Mr. Bannatine of the disaster, and he arrived in town almost simultaneously with Mr. McGregor, who was already on his way home when the murder occurred. As Mr. Bannatine is well acquainted with all the subsequent events, I prefer that he should give the account of our action since that time."

It was clearly very painful to Mr. Gordon to talk upon the subject of his nephew's murder, and Mr. Bannatine willingly took up the thread of the story. He had practiced at the bar so long that his style resembled that of a witness under examination, and he was always careful to give his authority whenever he stated facts outside of his own observation. His testimony was of the greatest importance to me, and I took very full notes as he went along.

CHAPTER II.

I RECEIVED the intelligence of George Gordon's murder about noon, by a messenger from Mr. Gordon. I immediately rode into town and went to the bank, where I arrived about two o'clock. The inquest was not completed, but at the sheriff's suggestion the jury adjourned until the next morning. The cause of death, according to the testimony of Dr. Hartman and Dr. Larimore, was concussion of the brain, produced by three separate blows on the back of the head; the blows might have been dealt with the canceling hammer, which, Mr. Gordon said, had been found close by the body. The latter was removed to the hotel preparatory to the funeral.

"Mr. Gordon, Mr. McGregor, and myself then proceeded to open the bank, taking the sheriff to assist us in searching for clues to aid in the detection of the criminals. We first opened all the shutters to give as much light as possible. We then examined the interior of the bank; outside of the counter nothing whatever was found, but inside we discovered several important traces of the murderer. The fireplace showed that something had recently been burned in it. The grate had been perfectly clean all summer, and Mr. Gordon tells me such was the case when he left the bank at four o'clock. The character of the ashes—as I am assured by expert chemists—denoted that clothing had been burned, and while examining them I found several buttons; here they are," he added, producing four or five iron buttons, and the charred remains of two or three horn buttons.

"While feeling around in the light ashes beneath the grate," continued Mr. Bannatine, "I found a piece of paper twisted up and charred at one end; its appearance indicated that it had been used to light the fire in the grate. On unrolling it carefully, it proved to be a fragment of a note for $927.78; the signature, part of the date, and the amount of the note were left uncharred, but most of the upper portion was wholly burned. The signature was that of Alexander P. Drysdale, our esteemed county clerk."

Mr. Bannatine here showed me this fragment pressed out between two oblong pieces of heavy plate glass. I glanced at it a few minutes, and then placed it beside the buttons for future examination.

"Among the few scraps of paper found," resumed Mr. Bannatine, "was another one, which we found under George's body, saturated with blood. The murderer had evidently destroyed every piece of paper that he could find; but this one had probably been lying on the floor, and when George fell, it was hidden by his body. This, and the note, were the only papers found on the desks or about the floor of the bank which had any writing upon them; even the waste paper baskets and their contents had been burned. Here is the paper, Mr. Pinkerton; we have preserved it carefully, because we thought that it might suggest something to a detective, though it had no special significance to us."

He handed me the paper, as he spoke. It was a fragment of letter paper, about three by six inches in size. It was stained a brownish red by poor young Gordon's life-blood; but beneath the stain, were plainly visible the pen marks of the murdered man. It had a number of figures on one side, arranged like examples in addition, though they were scattered carelessly, as if he had been checking off balances, and had used this fragment to verify his additions. The reverse side was blank. I laid this paper beside the note, and Mr. Bannatine continued his story:

"We then opened the safe, and counted the money; this was easily done, for we found that all the loose money was gone, leaving only a small quantity of coin and a number of packages of bills. These latter were put up in lots of five thousand dollars each, and were wrapped in a bright red tissue paper. George had put up over one hundred thousand dollars in this way, about a week before, and the murderer had not touched these packages at all: we were thus spared a loss, which would have somewhat crippled us. As it was, the loss in bills amounted to about one hundred and five thousand dollars, while exactly twenty-eight thousand dollars in gold eagles and double eagles, were also missing. A few days after the murder, one of Col. Garnett's slaves found two twenty-dollar gold pieces at an old fording place on Rocky Creek, just outside the city, and we came to the conclusion that the robber had dropped them there; but of course, we could not identify gold pieces, and so we could not be sure. The coroner closed the inquest the following day, and the jury found a verdict of death at the hands of a person or persons unknown. The funeral was attended by people from miles around, and there was a general determination shown to spare no pains to bring the murderers to justice; large rewards were offered by the Governor, by the bank, and by the county officials, and some of the best detectives in the country were employed, but all to no purpose. When the gold pieces were found, a number of George's intimate friends organized a party to search the adjoining woods for traces of the criminals, as it was thought they might have camped out in that vicinity, before or after the deed. All of George's intimate friends joined in the search, except Mr. Drysdale, who was so much overcome at the terrible occurrence, that he was quite prostrated. Nothing was found by this party, however; neither have the various detectives, professional and amateur, who have investigated the case, made the slightest progress toward a solution of the mystery. We have determined to make one more effort, Mr. Pinkerton, and therefore we have sent for you to aid us. It may be that you will see some trace which others have overlooked; you can take whatever steps you choose, and you need spare no expense. If you are successful, we will pay you liberally, besides the rewards offered."

"One of the rules of my Agency," I replied, " forbids the acceptance of rewards; hence, I wish it understood in advance, that my only charges will be according to my regular schedule of prices, and that I expect nothing more. This is my invariable custom, whether the case be one of murder, arson, burglary, or simple theft; the number of detectives, and the time they are employed, will determine the amount I shall charge."

We then arranged the financial portion of our agree-

ment to our mutual satisfaction, and I began my investi-
gations.

"What detectives have you hitherto employed, Mr.
Bannatine?" I asked.

"I first laid the matter before two New York detectives,
who had been highly recommended to me," he replied;
"but they could offer no satisfactory theory to work upon,
and after staying here three or four weeks, they said that
the murder must have been committed by some member
of a gang of gamblers; they thought the murderer would
probably go to New Orleans to exchange his money, and
that it would be easy to learn by going to that city,
whether any gambler had had an unusual amount of
money about that time. We were not very well satisfied
with this theory, and so the detectives returned to New
York. We next engaged two detectives from New
Orleans, but they were equally unsuccessful. We then
allowed the matter to rest until about a month ago, when
we heard such a favorable account of the manner in
which you had conducted a case of great difficulty, that
we began to discuss the propriety of engaging you in
investigating this affair. The more we heard of you, the
better we were satisfied, and finally, we authorized Mr.
McGregor to write to you on the subject."

"Well, Mr. Bannatine, I shall do my best," I replied,
"but you must not expect me to work miracles. Now, I
am going to ask you a number of questions, and I wish
you to answer them without regard to their apparent
drift. Who were George Gordon's intimate friends?"

"Mr. Flanders, Mr. Drysdale, Mr. Patterson, and Mr.

Henry Caruthers; I think they were the only ones he was really very intimate with; isn't it so, Mr. Gordon?"

"Yes; George had very few cronies," replied Mr. Gordon.

"Who is Mr. Caruthers?" I asked.

"He is the son of a wealthy planter living a few miles from town," replied Mr. Bannatine.

"Where was he the afternoon previous to the murder?"

"He came into the bank for a few minutes," said Mr. Gordon, "and asked George to spend Sunday with him on the plantation; then he rode home."

"Were there any strange men in or about the bank that day?"

"None, so far as we could learn; nearly every person that I can recollect having seen that day was a customer, or a townsman whom I knew."

"When George gave up carrying the safe keys home with him, where did he leave them?"

"There is a secret drawer in that desk, which opens by pressing this knob, thus," said Mr. McGregor, suiting the action to the word; "we used to keep the keys there."

"Did any one beside you four gentlemen know this hiding place?"

"I am sure that no one else knew it," said Mr. McGregor.

"Was it necessary for George to open the safe that night, or could he have done his work without going into the vault at all?"

"He had work to do on the journal and ledger, and he would have to use the keys to get them out of the vault.

He did not need to open the inner safe where the money was, however."

"Does the outer vault key open both doors?"

"No; but they were kept on the same chain for convenience."

"Were the ledger and journal on George's desk when you entered the bank, Mr. Gordon?"

"No, sir; they were put away in their usual places in the vault."

"Did they show any marks of blood?"

"None at all; they were perfectly clean."

. "Could you tell from their appearance whether George had done any work upon them that night?"

"Yes; I am sure he had done a great deal; in fact he had finished up all entries to date."

"Were there any papers missing besides the money?"

"Yes; one or two bundles of old checks, drafts, etc., were used to assist in burning the murderer's clothes. They were fastened in packages with fine wire, and we found the wire in the grate."

"Then this note, signed 'Alexander P. Drysdale,' might have been pulled out of one of these packages?"

"I suppose so; I don't know where else it came from; do you, Mr. McGregor?" said Mr. Gordon, rather bewildered.

"No; I never thought about where it came from," said Mr. McGregor. "I suppose the man built a fire of old papers and the fragments of the waste paper baskets, and then used that note to set them on fire from the lamp."

"There were no papers of any value used, then?" I continued.

"Oh, no; the papers were old bundles, merely kept as archives of the bank."

I then picked up the note and glanced at it; as I did so, something caught my eye which sent the blood throbbing through my veins at a feverish speed. Enough of the date remained to show that it was drawn some time during the year of the murder, hence it could hardly be one of the archives. Besides, a note, if paid, would be returned to the maker, canceled; if unpaid, it would be kept among the bills receivable, in the inner safe; in neither case could it have been stowed away among the old checks and drafts. This reasoning passed through my mind quickly, and I realized that that little piece of paper might play an important part in the tragedy after all. I did not form any definite theory on the instant, but still I had a sort of presentiment that I had touched a spring which might open the windows of this dark mystery and let in the light of day. I did not show what I thought to my companions, but continued to ask questions.

"Was Mr. Patterson in the bank the day of the murder, Mr. Gordon?"

"Oh, no; he was not in this part of the country at that time; he had been in Mobile for some weeks."

"I understood you to say that Mr. Flanders went no further than the private door with George; did he notice any one standing about when he came away?"

"No; he stopped only an instant, while George unlocked the door, and then gave the jewel box to him to put away. George wished him good night, with the remark that he could not ask him in, as he would be too busy to entertain him. Mr. Flanders then came straight back to my store; but he said at the inquest that he heard George lock the door behind him, and that he saw no one around the building."

"Do you know anything about his circumstances at that time? Was he in need of money?"

"No, indeed; he had a large balance to his credit. Why, surely, you do not see any reason to suspect Mr. Flanders?" said Mr. McGregor.

"I don't say that I suspect anybody," I replied, "but I wish to gather all the information possible. Now, please tell me how large a balance Mr. Flanders had on deposit."

Mr. McGregor immediately examined the ledger for the previous year, and reported that the balance due Mr. Flanders at the time of the murder, was over twelve thousand dollars.

"You see, Mr. Pinkerton," he went on to say, "we balanced our books up to that date, and thus we know just how each person's account stood that day."

"Well, did you find that any of those gentlemen, who were in the habit of entering the bank after business hours, were in debt to the bank, or that they were cramped for money at that time?" I asked, carelessly.

"None of them were in debt to the bank, I know," replied Mr. McGregor; "whether there were any of them in need of money particularly, I cannot say."

"Had any of them tried to borrow from the bank recently?"

"No; in fact, none of them had drawn out the balances due them."

"Please give me a list of their balances on that day," I said; "just give me a memorandum of the amounts standing to each one's credit."

"Whose accounts shall we give you?" asked Mr. McGregor, evidently wondering what object I had in view.

"Well, let me have those of Mr. Flanders, Mr. Patterson, Mr. Drysdale, and Mr. Caruthers; also, let me know whether any of those gentlemen had made any loan from the bank during that year, and if so, the amount, date, etc., and whether a note was given, or security of any kind."

Mr. McGregor, and the other two gentlemen, were completely mystified at my request, but they complied with my wishes, and I noted down the amounts given me in my note-book.

The balances were as follows: Patterson, $2,472.27; Drysdale, $324.22; Caruthers, $817.48; and Flanders, $12,263.03. None of them had made loans from the bank, except Caruthers, who had once overdrawn his account nearly three hundred dollars, but he gave no note, as he was good for any amount. None of the others had given a note to the bank, or to any one else, so far as was known, for several years.

"Now, gentlemen," I said, "please take me into the bank and show me exactly how the place appeared when Mr. Gordon first discovered that George had been murdered."

Mr. Gordon rose with great effort and opened the door connecting the private office with the main bank. It was evidently very painful to him, but he did not shrink. Turning to me, he said:

"Mr. Pinkerton, let Mr. McGregor go first, and light the lamp; I will then proceed just as I did that morning, and will point out the exact position of everything in the bank."

Mr. McGregor accordingly lighted a large lamp, which threw a soft radiance over the whole interior, and the two moved the furniture into the position in which it had been found on that fatal morning. Mr. Gordon then showed me the exact position of the body, the spot where the paper lay, the canceling hammer, and the blood-marks. After I had been shown everything, I stood and thought over the matter in connection with the surroundings, and endeavored to re-enact the scene of the murder in my own mind. Bit by bit, I brought out some of the surroundings to my own satisfaction, and when I went back to the private office, I had a well-defined theory in my mind. Not that I had so narrowed down my suspicions, as to fix them upon any particular individual — I had not yet gone so far — but my theory was fully established, and I felt sure that by working it up carefully, I should soon discover some traces of the guilty party. The officers of the bank followed me in silence, and on resuming our seats, I said:

"Gentlemen, I wish to take a day to weigh the testimony in this case, before I can give you any opinion about it. I would like to take this note, the memorandum, and the buttons to my room, and to-morrow evening I will tell you what conclusions I have reached. Is that satisfactory?"

3

"Certainly; we do not wish to proceed in haste, Mr. Pinkerton," said Mr. Bannatine; "we will meet you then at the same hour to-morrow."

"I do not wish to seem impatient," said Mr. Gordon, "but can you not tell me now whether you have obtained any clue from what we have told you, which will enable you to learn more?"

Mr. Gordon's anxiety was so keen that I wished to relieve his mind somewhat; but, on the other hand, I did not wish to raise his hopes unnecessarily, lest some unforeseen thing might occur to overthrow my theory entirely. I replied, therefore:

"Mr. Gordon, I may think I have a clue now, which, on mature reflection, may prove worthless; hence, I should prefer to take a day, before giving my opinion."

"You are right, Mr. Pinkerton," he said; "I should feel worse to have my hopes raised, only to be dashed down again, than if I had never expected anything. Take your own time, and then let us know the result."

"There are two questions more, which I would like answered," I said. "Was it possible for any person to have entered the bank by force? That is, were there any indications whatever, to show that the murderer might have possibly gained entrance during George's absence at dinner?"

"No; none at all. The sheriff made a very careful examination of all the windows, and both doors," replied Mr. McGregor. "He thought that a gang of gamblers, who stopped here a few weeks, might have used nippers on the key of the side door after George had locked it, and that they had then stolen upon George, at his desk, and killed him; but, there were no evidences that such was the case."

"Well, did any one, except you three gentlemen, know the private signal by which those inside the bank could tell that the person at the door, was one of the bank officers?"

"I am not sure about that," said Mr. Gordon; "possibly some of our well-known friends might have been with us when we gained admittance to the bank, but I cannot say that I think they ever learned the signal."

"You think, however, that Patterson, Drysdale, Flanders, or Caruthers, *might* have known it?"

"Yes; in fact, on thinking it over, I feel quite sure that Mr. Patterson and Mr. Drysdale did know it."

"Well, I don't think I have any more questions to ask," I said. "I shall be here promptly at eight o'clock to-morrow evening, and if you should wish to communicate with me before that time, send me a message, and I will call at the bank. This will not attract attention, as my business is supposed to be cotton buying, and a visit at the bank will not be considered unusual."

I then took charge of the papers, etc., and went to my room at the hotel. I merely glanced at the buttons, and bank note, hastily, as I knew they could serve only as corroboratory evidence in the event of obtaining a weak chain of proof. I then turned to the note, which I studied long and carefully. I was convinced that it was of recent date, at the time of the murder, although only the last figure of the date was visible. I finally looked over the blood-stained piece of paper, which George had nearly covered with figures. I saw at a glance, that there was no reading matter on it, but I began to go over his figures half mechanically, mentally following his addition, to verify it.

Suddenly my eyes caught two numbers near the bottom of the paper. They were placed together, and their difference was written below; they were much fainter than the rest, having been made in pencil, instead of in ink. It was probably due to this fact, that they had never been noticed before, as the deep stain made it difficult to distinguish them clearly, without close observation. However that may be, they acted upon me like an electric shock, and I was obliged to walk about the room a few minutes, to compose my nerves. It was strange that those faint lines should have told so much, but it seemed almost, as if the murdered man had whispered his murderer's name to me. The numbers which were there set down were $927.78, and $324.22. *One of them was the amount of the half burned note of Drysdale; the other, was the amount of his balance in the bank.*

I sat up until a very late hour, thinking over the possible solution of the mystery, and when I finally went to bed, I had satisfied myself as to the identity of the murderer. The next day, I rose late, and spent the afternoon in arranging the points of evidence in consecutive order, so as to be able to present them to the bank officials in the most convincing manner. I tnen walked around town for exercise. During my walk, I visited Mr. Flanders' jewelry store and the county clerk's office.

Mr. Flanders was an elderly gentlemen of very mild and courteous manners, and his whole appearance would lead any one to regard it as impossible, that he should have committed murder.

Mr. Drysdale, the county clerk, was a fine looking man, of about forty years of age. He was of the nervous, sanguine type; was quiet and courteous, but haughty and reserved to strangers; he was looking thin and weary, as if he worked too hard, and streaks of gray were just visible in his hair and mustache.

I talked with him for about half an hour, representing that I was a stranger, desirous of gaining information about the plantations of the county. He answered my questions politely, but as briefly as possible, and I saw that my presence, apparently, bored him, and interfered with his duties. As I was about to go, I asked him to write the name and address of some reliable cotton factor in my note-book, and he complied very willingly. I then returned to the hotel, and patiently waited until eight o'clock.

CHAPTER III.

O N going to the bank I found the three gentlemen
awaiting me most anxiously. After the usual
greeting we seated ourselves at the table. I arranged my
notes for convenient reference, and began to state my
conclusions:

"Gentlemen, I have approached this case with a great
deal of care, and have given it much thought. Aside
from the importance of the interests involved, there are
other reasons which render me cautious in forming and
stating an opinion; other detectives of ability and experience have been baffled; several months have elapsed
since the crimes were committed; and, lastly, the theory
upon which I have reasoned has led me in such a direction that nothing but the strongest conviction in my own
mind would warrant me in making the statement which I
am now about to give you. Let me first, then, review the
case, and show the chain of evidence as it appears to me:

"George Gordon appears to have been a young man
of more than average ability as a bank officer; he was
cautious in his habits, and at this particular time he had
recently been specially cautioned by Mr. McGregor;
consequently it is likely that he would have been unusually careful to admit only those with whom he was very
well acquainted. Again, the position of the furniture and
the appearance of the blood-marks, show that George

31

was standing at his desk, and that he was struck from behind. Now, he had finished his work on the books and put them away. What, then, was he doing? There is but one thing which throws any light upon this subject —the bank bill which you found in his hand. From its presence I infer that he was engaged in handling money; indeed, I may say that he must have been either receiving it or paying it out. That he was receiving it is not likely, for the murderer was probably short of funds; hence I conclude that he was paying it out. It is also clear that the amount must have been large, as shown by the denomination of the bill—one hundred dollars.

"These facts and inferences lead me to believe that the murderer was a personal friend of George, and a customer of the bank; and I may say that I had reached this conclusion yesterday evening, while listening to the testimony of you three gentlemen, before I had discovered any corroborative evidence. I will now give some of the additional points which I have brought out since then; but I wish that you would first tell me whether this signature is genuine," I said, pointing to Alexander P. Drysdale's name on the note.

"Oh, yes; there is no doubt of that," said Mr. McGregor; "I am perfectly familiar with his signature, and there is no question in my mind but that he signed that himself."

"Well, gentlemen, I will now make up a possible case, and you can see how nearly it compares with the present matter. I will suppose that a man of wealth, refinement, and position, should become cramped for money to supply present necessities; he is intimate with the officers of a wealthy bank; he goes there one evening and is admitted by his friend, the acting cashier. He explains his embarrassment, and his friend agrees to lend him the amount which he requires. The friend completes his work, puts away his books, and figures up the amount needed. The borrower has a small balance to his credit, and he gives a note for the difference. Then the teller opens the safe, brings out a roll of bills, and begins to count out the amount. The safe door is left open, and the visitor sees within the piles of bank-notes and the rouleaux of gold. A fortune in cash is within his grasp with only a human life standing in his way; his perplexities and embarrassments come upon him with added force as he sees the means before him by which he may escape their power to annoy him. Like Tantalus, dying of thirst with the water at his very lips, this man gazes on the wealth piled up in that safe. Glancing around, he sees his friend slowly counting the paltry hundreds he is to receive; close by lies a heavy weapon, heretofore used for innocent business purposes; another glance into the safe and insanity is upon him; his brain is a perfect hell of contending passions; again the thought flashes into his mind—'Only a life between me and that money.' He seizes the heavy hammer and deals his victim a terrible blow behind the ear; as the latter falls lifeless, the murderer strikes him twice more to make sure that there shall be no witnesses to testify in the case. The deed is done, and there remains nothing to prevent him from seizing the contents of the safe. But first, he must protect himself from the danger of discovery; to this end he carefully removes his bloody clothing, gathers every vestige of paper within

sight, and breaks up the waste paper baskets for fuel.
He needs more flame, however, and he takes several
packages of old papers to make the fire fiercer; then his
eye falls on a slip of paper lying on the desk, and he
twists it nervously into a lighter to convey fire from the
lamp to the mass of material in the fire-place. The flame
is started, and soon the clothes are reduced to ashes.
Stealthily he packs the packages of bills and the rolls
of coin, and when he has taken as much as he can carry,
he slips noiselessly away, leaving no trace of his identity.
No one has seen him enter or depart ; his position is far
above the reach of suspicion ; every clue has been
destroyed in the fire-place, and no witness to his guilt
can possibly be raised up. So he thinks ; and as month
after month passes, as detective after detective abandons
the case in despair, as the excitement dies out in the
public mind, and as the friends of the deceased apparently give up the hopeless task of seeking for the murderer, his confidence becomes complete, and he no longer
fears detection.

"But stop ! when his victim fell a bloody corpse at his
feet, *was* every witness destroyed ? No, gentlemen ;
helpless and lifeless as that body fell, it yet had the power
to avenge itself. The right hand convulsively grasps a
bank note, and it is hidden from sight by the position
assumed in falling ; a slip of white paper dotted with
figures at random, is also covered, and is quickly saturated with blood ; a fragment of paper is found below the
grate, twisted so tightly as to have burned only in part ;
lastly, the direction of the blood-spirts show that the first
blow was struck on the left side. Now, gentlemen, do

you think you can read the testimony of these dumb witnesses?"

"My God! I do not know what to think," said Mr. Gordon.

"I see where your suspicions lead," said Mr. Bannatine, "but I do not yet fully know whether I can see the evidence in the same light that you do. Please go on and tell us all you suspect, and your reasons."

"Yes, Mr. Pinkerton," said Mr. McGregor, "whom do you suspect?"

"Gentlemen," I replied, solemnly, "I have formed no hasty conclusion in this matter, and I should not accuse any man without the strongest reasons for believing him guilty; but I think that when I have connected together the links which I have gathered, you will agree with me in the moral certainty that George Gordon was murdered by Alexander P. Drysdale, and no other."

"Go on, go on, Mr. Pinkerton," said Mr. Gordon, in great excitement. "It seems impossible, yet there are some slight fancies in my mind which seem to confirm that theory. Tell us all your conclusions, and how you have arrived at them."

"Well, first, I am satisfied that only a particular friend would have been admitted to the bank by George that night; second, the blow was struck from behind, on the left side, showing that the murderer was probably left-handed. Mr. Drysdale satisfies both of these conditions; I visited him to-day and saw him write an address in my note-book with his left hand. Third, I have here a note for $927.78, signed 'Alexander P. Drysdale;' the signature, you say, is genuine, and further, you told me yesterday that you had not held a note of Mr. Drysdale's for some years. On reflection you will see that this note could not have been taken from the packages of bank archives which were burned, for it never could have been put there; moreover it is dated '1856,' and must have been made some time last year. As you have no record of such a note, I infer that it was drawn the night of the murder. Fourthly, I have conclusive evidence of that fact in this slip of blood-stained paper," and so saying, I produced the slip upon which George had done his figuring.

" How! where!" exclaimed my listeners.

" Near the bottom of that paper you will find in light pencil marks three numbers arranged like an example in subtraction, while the rest are all additions in ink. The figures are: first, 1,252.00; then, 324.22; and 927.78 below the line. Mr. Drysdale's balance was $324.22, and the amount of this note bearing his signature is $927.78. It looks to me as if he wanted to draw $1,252.00, and that George subtracted the amount of his balance in bank, $324.22, from the amount he wished to draw, $1,252.00, and that Mr. Drysdale then gave his note for the difference, $927.78. What do you think of my witness, gentlemen?"

The three gentlemen put their heads together over the paper long enough to convince themselves that the figures were really there, and then they resumed their seats in silence. I had watched their faces carefully as I drew my conclusions, and had seen their expressions change from incredulity to uncertainty, then to amazement, finally turning gradually to half belief; but when they sat down, positive conviction was evident in every face.

"How is it possible that these facts were never discovered before?" ejaculated Mr. Bannatine.

"It is very simple," I replied; "the search has hitherto been conducted on a wrong basis. The whole endeavor seems to have been to *guess* who might have done the deed, and then to find evidence to convict him. My plan in all similar cases is, to first examine the evidence before me, with a perfectly unbiased mind; then, having formed a theory by reasoning on general principles, as applied to the facts in my possession, I proceed to look about for some person who will answer the conditions of my theory. I may find more than one, and I then am obliged to make each such person the object of my attention until I obtain convincing proof of his innocence or guilt. The person upon whom my theory causes suspicion to fall, may have been hitherto regarded as above suspicion; but, that fact does not deter me in the least degree from placing that person's circumstances, motives, and actions under the microscope, so to speak; for experience and observation, have taught me that the most difficult crimes to fix upon the criminal, are those which have been committed by men whose previous reputation had been unspotted. Now, you have never connected Mr. Drysdale with this affair, because it has never entered your minds to suspect him; but, had you gone over the ground in the same manner that I have done, you would have been led to the same conclusion. This is the real point, where the services of an experienced detective, are most valuable. The plan by which a detective operation is to be conducted, is as important as the method of procedure. To find a man who is hiding from justice, his criminality being well known, is a task of little difficulty, compared with the labor involved in mysterious cases, where there is apparently, nothing left to identify the criminal. I claim no special credit in this case, since the clues have proven more numerous than had been supposed, but I have given you my idea of the proper way to conduct an investigation, simply to show you how I am accustomed to work. Let me now ask, whether any of you have doubts, as to the propriety of putting my detectives upon the trail of Mr. Drysdale, to determine the extent of his connection, if any, in the murder of George Gordon?"

"None whatever," said Mr. Bannatine, emphatically; "it seems almost impossible that he should be guilty; but, in the face of the strong array of accusing circumstances cited by you, Mr. Pinkerton, I can only say: 'Go on with your work in your own way.' The innocent have nothing to fear, and the guilty deserve no mercy."

"Amen," said both the other gentlemen.

"What is your plan?" asked Mr. Gordon.

"Well, gentlemen," I replied, "I have been struck with some strong points of resemblance between Drysdale and one of Bulwer's characters, Eugene Aram. You are aware, that the only evidence we can bring against Drysdale, is circumstantial, and that we could hardly obtain an indictment on the strength of it; still less a conviction for murder. Besides, there is a large amount of money at stake, and it is desirable to recover that money, as well as to convict the murderer. We must proceed, therefore, with great caution, lest we defeat our own plans by premature action. I have arranged a scheme to obtain a direct proof of Drysdale's guilt, and with your consent, I will put it in operation immediately."

I then gave the details of my plan, and the gentlemen, though somewhat nervous as to the result, finally acquiesced in it.

The next morning, I left Atkinson, for Chicago, where I duly arrived, somewhat improved in health, by my Southern trip. I immediately sent for Timothy Webster, one of my most expert detectives, to whom I gave full charge of the case in Atkinson. I explained to him all the circumstances connected with it, and instructed him in the plan I had arranged. Mrs. Kate Warne, and a young man named Green, were assigned to assist Webster, and all the necessary disguises and clothing, were prepared at short notice.

Mrs. Warne was the first lady whom I had ever employed, and this was one of the earliest operations in which she was engaged. As a detective, she had no superior, and she was a lady of such refinement, tact, and discretion, that I never hesitated to entrust to her some of my most difficult undertakings.

It will be understood by the reader, that each detective made daily reports to me, and that I constantly directed the operation by mail or telegraph. This has always been my invariable custom, and no important steps are ever taken without my order, unless circumstances should occur which would not admit the delay.

CHAPTER IV.

A BOUT a week after my departure from Atkinson, a gentleman arrived there by the evening train, and went to the hotel. He was an intelligent, shrewd, agreeable business man, about thirty-five years old, and he impressed all who made his acquaintance, as a gentleman of ability and energy. He signed the register, as ' John M. Andrews, Baltimore,' and the landlord soon learned from him that he had come to Atkinson to reside permanently, if he could get into business there. Mr. Andrews was evidently a man of considerable wealth, though he made no ostentatious display, nor did he talk about his property as though he cared to impress upon other people the idea that he was rich. Still, it came to be generally understood, in a few days, that he had made quite a fortune, as a cotton broker, in Baltimore, and that he had a considerable sum in cash to invest, when a desirable opportunity should offer. This fact, together with his agreeable manners, made his society quite an acquisition to the town, and he was soon on familiar terms with all the regular boarders in the hotel, and with many prominent residents of the place.

Some days after Mr. Andrews arrived the hotel received another equally popular guest. She gave her name, as Mrs. R. C. Potter, and her object in visiting Atkinson, was to improve her health. She was accompanied by her father, Mr. C. B. Rowell, a fine looking, white-haired old gentleman, but he remained only long enough to see her comfortably settled, and then returned to their home in Jacksonville, Florida, as his business required his immediate presence there. Mrs. Potter was a distingushed looking brunette; she was a widow with no children, and she might have passed for thirty years of age. She was tall and graceful, and her entertaining conversation made her a general favorite among the ladies in the hotel. She was not an invalid, strictly speaking, but the family physician had recommended that she should go to the dry air of northern Mississippi for a few months, to escape the rainy, foggy weather of Florida at that season.

About a week after her arrival, she went out with two other ladies, Mrs. Townsend and Mrs. Richter, to explore the beauties of Rocky Creek. They spent a pleasant afternoon in the wooded ravines, and it was after five o'clock, before they returned. As they sauntered down one of the pleasantest streets of the town, they noticed a lady standing at the gate of an elegant residence, with large grounds.

"Oh! there is Mrs. Drysdale," said Mrs Townsend. "Have you met her, Mrs. Potter?"

"Not yet, though I have heard of her so frequently, that I feel almost as if I knew her."

"Well, I think you will like each other very much," said Mrs. Richter, "and we will introduce you to her."

On reaching the gate, therefore, the ladies presented Mrs. Potter in due form.

"I have been intending to call on you, Mrs. Potter,"

said Mrs. Drysdale, "but my youngest child has not been well, and I have not gone anywhere for several weeks. In fact, I am quite a home body at all times, and I always expect my friends to waive ceremony, and visit me a great deal more than I visit them. I hope you will not wait for me, Mrs. Potter, for my domestic affairs keep me very busy just now; I shall be glad to see you any time that you feel like dropping in."

"I shall be very glad to dispense with formalities," answered Mrs. Potter, "and you can depend upon seeing me soon."

After some further conversation, the three ladies resumed their homeward walk, leaving Mrs. Drysdale still waiting for her husband. He was soon seen by the ladies, rapidly walking up the street toward his home. He was on the opposite side, so that he merely bowed to them, and hastened on.

"There seems to have been quite a change in Mr. Drysdale during the last year," said Mrs. Richter. "My husband was speaking of it the other day. He said that Drysdale was becoming really unsociable. I hope he is not growing dissipated, for the sake of his wife, who is a lovely woman."

"Yes; she seems to be a most devoted wife and mother," said Mrs. Potter. "Possibly, the change in Mr. Drysdale, is due to business troubles."

"Oh, no; that is impossible," said Mrs. Townsend; "he is very wealthy indeed, and as he is not engaged in any regular business, he cannot be financially embarrassed. No, I attribute his recent peculiarities, to religious doubts; he has not been to church since last fall."

4

"Is it as long as that?" asked Mrs. Richter.

"Yes; I recollect it, because he did not go to the funeral of poor George Gordon, and he has not attended service since then."

"Well, if he really is in religious trouble, the minister ought to visit him and give him advice," said Mrs. Richter.

As they walked toward the hotel, they turned the conversation into a different channel without reaching any conclusion as to the cause of Mr. Drysdale's eccentricities.

A few days thereafter Mrs. Potter called upon Mrs. Drysdale and passed the afternoon very pleasantly. When Mr. Drysdale came home he was very polite and agreeable; he seemed glad to find his wife enjoying herself, and when Mrs. Potter rose to go, both husband and wife urged her warmly to come frequently.

"I am going out to my plantation in a day or two," said Mr. Drysdale, "and I hope you will visit my wife while I am gone, as I am afraid she may be lonesome."

"Who are you going with?" asked Mrs. Drysdale.

"There is a gentleman from Baltimore, staying at the hotel," replied Mr. Drysdale, "and he talks of investing some money in land, so I thought I would take him out to see Bristed's old place next to mine. It is going to ruin now, but if a man like Mr. Andrews would take it, he could make it pay. He seems very intelligent and agreeable; I suppose you have met him, Mrs. Potter?"

"Oh, yes; he was introduced to me the first week I was here," replied Mrs. Potter. "He seems to me to be a Southern gentleman with a good deal of real Yankee shrewdness."

"That is my opinion, also," said Mr. Drysdale, "and if he buys Bristed's place, he will join me in some improvements which are much needed."

"Well, good afternoon, Mrs. Drysdale," said Mrs. Potter; "I am going out horseback riding in a day or two, and perhaps I will stop here a few minutes on my way back."

"Do so, Mrs. Potter; we shall be delighted to see you. Good afternoon."

On Mrs. Potter's return to the hotel, she stayed in the parlor for some time, and as Mr. Andrews came in soon after, they had a pleasant *tete-a-tete* before going to dinner.

The next morning Mr. Andrews went out to get a cabinet-maker to make a small book-case for his room, and the hotel clerk directed him to the shop of Mr. Breed. The latter said that he was very busy, indeed, but that he could get a young man who was boarding with him to do the job.

"Is he a good workman?" asked Mr. Andrews.

"I think he is," replied Breed, "though I am not sure, as he came here only day before yesterday from Memphis. He has served his time at the trade, however, and he ought to be able to make a book-case neatly."

"Well, send him over, Mr. Breed, and I will give him a trial. By the way, who was that gentleman that just passed? I have seen him several times, but have never met him in society."

"That was Mr. Peter A. Gordon," said Breed. "He boards at the hotel, also, but he rarely mingles with other men except in business."

"I am surprised at that," Mr. Andrews remarked, "for

he appears like a naturally genial man; yet he has a very
sad look."

" Yes; he has never recovered from the shock of his
nephew's murder last fall; he always used to be very
sociable and hospitable, but now he seems too much cast
down to care for society. You may have heard of the
dreadful manner in which young George Gordon was
murdered ?"

" Oh, yes; I recollect," said Mr. Andrews; " the circumstances were related to me soon after I arrived here.
George Gordon seems to have been a fine young fellow,
and I don't wonder the old gentleman mourns his loss."

" He was one of the most promising young men I ever
knew," said Mr. Breed, warmly; "and speaking of poor
George, reminds me that I noticed a strong resemblance
to him in this young workman boarding with me. Ordi-
narily I would not have perceived it, but yesterday he
slipped on a coat of mine, which was just like the one
George used to wear, and the likeness was remarkable."

" You were one of the first at the bank the day after
the murder, were you not, Mr. Breed ?"

"Yes; and it was a dreadful sight. It was wonderful
how Mr. Peter Gordon retained his presence of mind;
he did not break down until he found that there was no
hope of discovering the murderer."

" Was no one ever suspected ?" asked Mr. Andrews.

"Oh, yes; several persons were arrested—gamblers
and loafers—but they all proved their innocence conclu-
sively."

Mr. Andrews showed considerable interest in the

murder, and **Mr.** Breed related all that was known about it. When he was about to go, Mr. Andrews said :

"Well, it is a very mysterious affair, and I am not surprised that Mr. Gordon is so dejected; that horrible scene must be always before him. By the way, don't let your young man dress in gray, when he comes to my room; I should be continually haunted with a suspicion that it was a ghost."

"Please don't speak of that to any one," said Mr. Breed, confidentially; "I ought not to have mentioned it myself, for young Green was frightened nearly out of his wits about it. As I said before, when he wears his every-day clothes, no one would notice any special resemblance, but in that particular style of dress, the likeness was really alarming. He was so scared, that in future, he will take great care not to be seen in any clothes like those of poor George."

"Of course, I shall not mention the matter," said **Mr.** Andrews; "send him over this afternoon."

CHAPTER V.

ON leaving Mr. Breed, Mr. Andrews paid a visit to Mr. Drysdale, at the latter's office.

"I hope I shall not interfere with your work, Mr. Drysdale," he said. "I am an idler for the present, but I try to respect the business hours of others, and so, if I disturb you, let me know it."

"Oh! not at all, I assure you," said Mr. Drysdale, warmly. "I am never very busy, and just now, there is nothing whatever to do. Indeed, I wish I had more to do — this lack of steady work wears upon me. I need something to keep my mind constantly occupied."

"That is where you and I differ," said Andrews; "I have worked pretty hard for twenty years, and now I am willing to take a rest. I don't wish to be wholly idle, but I like to give up a good part of my time to recreation."

"I used to feel so, too," said Drysdale, as if his thoughts were far away; then, he added, hastily, as if recollecting himself: "I mean that I have felt so at times, but I always need to come back to hard work again. Will you be ready to go out to my plantation next Monday?"

"Yes; Monday will suit me as well as any other day," replied Andrews. "When shall we return?"

"I had not intended to remain there more than three

or four days, unless you should wish to stay longer. If agreeable to you, we will return Thursday afternoon."

"That will enable me to join our riding party the next day," said Andrews. "All right; I will be ready to start Monday morning. Now, I must be going; I only stopped to find out when you would be ready to go."

"I am sorry you cannot stay longer," said Drysdale. "I hope that you will drop in without ceremony, whenever you feel like it."

In the afternoon, young Green, the cabinet-maker, called upon Mr. Andrews, and went up to the latter's room. The work to be done, must have required a great deal of explanation, as Green remained nearly an hour. As he went out, Mr. Andrews said to him:

"If we fail to return Thursday, you must be there Friday at the same hour. You had better take a look at the place before then."

On Monday, Mr. Drysdale called at the hotel immediately after breakfast, and found Mr. Andrews all ready for the ride to the plantation. As they rode out of town, Mr. Drysdale's spirits seemed to rise rapidly, and he entertained his companion so successfully, that when they reached the plantation, they had become quite well acquainted with each other. Drysdale was a man of fine education, and fascinating manners; he really had great eloquence, and his abilities were far above the average, but the circumstances of his life had not been such as to develop his powers, and give play to his ambition; hence, he was apparently becoming disappointed, sour, and morose. At least, this was the impression which many of his friends had gained, and they accounted for the gradual change in his manners on the above theory; namely, that he was the victim of disappointed ambition.

During their stay at the plantation, the gentlemen usually spent their evenings together, while the mornings were given up to business by Drysdale, and to hunting by Andrews. The plantation required a great deal of attention just in the spring, and Drysdale's time was pretty well occupied. Andrews easily formed the acquaintance of the neighboring planters, and he spent much of his time in paying visits around the country. He thought quite favorably of buying the Bristed plantation, as Drysdale had hoped, but the owner wished to sell another place with it, and Andrews did not care to buy both. Drysdale suggested that by autumn, the owner would be willing to sell it separately, and he advised Andrews to hold off until then.

On Thursday, Andrews started out shooting early, agreeing to be back at noon, to make an early start for Atkinson, as the time required to ride there, was about four hours. He strayed so far away, however, that it was two o'clock before he returned, and they did not mount their horses until three o'clock. By this time, they had become much more intimate than one would have expected on so short acquaintance, and Drysdale showed a marked pleasure in the company of his new friend. During the first part of the ride, he was as brilliant and entertaining as possible, but, as they approached the town, he began to lose his cheerfulness, and to become almost gloomy. Both gentlemen were rather tired, and they soon allowed the conversation to drop almost wholly.

It was early dusk when they reached the banks of Rocky Creek, about a mile from Drysdale's house. From this point, the scenery was bold and picturesque; the road passed through heavy masses of timber at times, and crossed many ravines and rocky gorges, as it followed the general direction of the winding stream. Daylight was rapidly fading into the night, though objects could still be distinguished quite well at a distance of one hundred yards. As they arrived at one of the wooded hillocks, over which the road passed, they were shut out from any very extended view, except in one direction. Here, Andrews reined in his horse a moment, to take a last look at the beauty of the scene, while Drysdale passed on a few yards in advance.

The spot was rather wild and perhaps a little weird; on the right was a dense forest, rising some distance above the road, which curved around the hill-side about mid-way to the crest; on the left the hill descended rapidly to the creek, along which ran a heavy belt of timber, which permitted only an occasional gleam of water to be seen; the abrupt hill-side between the road and the timber was nearly cleared of undergrowth, but it was filled with large boulders and creeping vines; over the tops of the timber the country stretched away in dissolving views as the mists of night began to form and spread over the landscape. Having paused an instant, Andrews spurred his horse forward just as Drysdale uttered an exclamation of horror. As he came up, he saw that Drysdale had stopped and was holding his reins in a convulsive grasp; all color was gone from his face, and he was trembling violently.

"What is the matter, Drysdale?" said Andrews, drawing up beside him.

"My God! look there!" broke from Drysdale's ashy lips, as he pointed down the hill-side.

At the distance of about fifty yards the figure of a young man was moving down the slope toward the timber. He walked slowly on, with a measured pace, turning his eyes neither to the right nor left. He was apparently about twenty-five or twenty-six years of age, and his face was indicative of intelligence, ability and energy. His course was nearly parallel to the direction of the road at that point, and only his profile could be seen. He wore a business suit of light gray clothes, but he had no hat on his head, and his curly hair was tossed lightly by the evening breeze. As he moved further from the road, the back of his head was more directly exposed, presenting a most ghastly sight. The thick brown locks were matted together in a mass of gore, and large drops of blood slowly trickled down upon his coat; the whole back of the skull seemed to be crushed in, while the deadly pallor of his face gave him the appearance of a corpse.

Drysdale seemed to rally his faculties a moment and shouted in powerful but hoarse tones:

"Say! you, sir! Who are you, and where are you going?"

Although his voice might have been heard at a long distance, the figure continued its course without indicating, even by a sign, that he had heard the hail.

"Why, what in the devil has got into you. Drysdale?"

"My God! look there!" broke from Drysdale's ashy lips, as he pointed down the hill-side.

asked Andrews. "Whom are you shouting at in such a savage way?"

"Don't you see that man down the hill?" he asked, in a perfect agony of fear and excitement. "See! right in line with that pointed rock; why, he is only a few yards off. My God! it can't be possible that you don't see him!"

"Upon my word, Drysdale," said Andrews, "if you keep on, I shall think you are going crazy. What man are you talking about? There is no one in sight, and either you are trying to play a joke on me, or else your imagination is most unpleasantly active."

"Andrews, look where I point, less than ten rods off," said Drysdale, in a hoarse whisper, clutching Andrews by the arm; "do you mean to say that you don't see a man slowly walking toward the creek?"

"I mean to say," replied Andrews, deliberately, "that there is no man in sight from here, either on that hill-side or any where else."

"God help me," muttered Drysdale, as the figure disappeared in the woods, "then it must have been a ghost."

"My dear fellow," said Andrews, sympathizingly, as they continued their ride, "I am afraid you are feverish; you probably imagined you saw something, and you are superstitious about the matter because I did not see it. Tell me what it was."

By this time they had passed some distance beyond the spot where Drysdale had seen the apparition, and he began to recover his strength somewhat. It was evident that he was still very much distressed, but he endeavored to pass the matter over.

"Oh! it was nothing of any consequence," he said, "but I thought I saw a man crossing that clearing."

"Well, what of it?" asked Andrews. "Was he a dangerous looking fellow?"

"Yes; very dangerous looking, indeed;" then, suddenly, as if struck by a plausible idea, he added: "I thought it was a negro with a gun; you know what my opinions are about allowing the slaves to have fire-arms, and this fellow looked like such a villain that I was really alarmed. You are sure you saw no one?"

"Quite sure," replied Andrews. "I am afraid you have worked too hard, and that you are going to be ill. I shall tell your wife to nurse you well for a few days to cure you of seeing spooks and wild niggers roaming 'round with guns."

"No, indeed," said Drysdale, hastily; "please say nothing to my wife; it would only alarm her unnecessarily."

"Well, take my advice and rest awhile," said Andrews. "Your nerves are a little shaken, and you will certainly be ill if you keep on working so steadily."

Drysdale soon relapsed into moody silence, and when they reached his gate, he was a really pitiable object. He asked Andrews to take supper with him, but as the invitation was given only as a matter of form, the latter excused himself, and rode immediately to the hotel. He happened to meet Mrs. Potter in the parlor, but he stopped only a few minutes to talk to her, as he was too hungry and tired to feel like entertaining the fascinating widow.

It was then only about seven o'clock, and Mrs. Potter

proposed to Mrs. Townsend, and several other ladies and gentlemen, that they take a walk. Accordingly, they strolled through the pleasant streets, enjoying the balmy spring air, and often stopping at the gates of their friends, to chat a few minutes. As they passed the Drysdale place, Mrs. Potter said:

"I want to run in to speak to Mrs. Drysdale a minute; I promised to stop here on our riding excursion to-morrow, but as it is postponed, I want to tell her not to expect me."

The rest of the party stayed at the gate, while Mrs. Potter went in. She was ushered into the library, and Mrs. Drysdale came down at once. Having explained her object in calling, Mrs. Potter asked whether Mr. and Mrs. Drysdale would not join the party outside, for a short walk.

"I am sorry to say, that my husband is quite unwell," said Mrs. Drysdale. "He returned from the plantation to-day, quite feverish, and excited, and now he is in a sort of nervous delirium. He has had one or two attacks before, but none so serious as this."

"I sincerely hope he is not going to be ill," said Mrs. Potter. "What does the doctor think?"

"Oh! he won't have a doctor," replied Mrs. Drysdale; "he says that I am the best doctor he can have, because I can soothe him."

Just then, Mrs. Potter heard a heavy footstep, beginning to pace up and down overhead.

"There, he has arisen,' said Mrs. Drysdale, "and I shall find him pacing the room, and muttering to himself like a crazy man. You must excuse me, as I must go to quiet him."

"Oh, certainly; I am sorry I called you away. Please let me know if I can do anything for you. If Mr. Drysdale should be seriously ill, don't be afraid to call upon me. I am an excellent nurse, and nothing would give me greater pleasure than to assist you; or, at least, I could look after the children."

"You are very kind, Mrs. Potter, and I shall be glad to accept your assistance, especially, as the children are so fond of you; however, I hope Aleck's illness will be only temporary."

Mrs. Potter then withdrew, and the party slowly strolled back to the hotel.

As Mrs. Drysdale surmised, her husband's illness was very brief, and in two or three days, he returned to his duties at the court house. He was somewhat changed in looks, however, his face being haggard, his figure slightly bowed, and his hand tremulous. He seemed, more than ever before, to avoid society, and on his way to the court house, he always chose the least frequented streets. The change in his looks and manners, was noticed only by a few who had formerly been intimate with him; in this little circle, his eccentricities were accounted for by significant gestures of drinking, and it was understood among those who knew him best, that liquor was responsible for the ruin of another fine fellow.

One peculiarity that he evinced was, a great partiality for the society of Mr. Andrews, and for the next week, they were together every day. He frequently referred, in conversation with Andrews, to the freak his imagination had played, while returning from the plantation, and, though Andrews always made light of it, and laughed at him, he evidently thought about it a great deal. It seemed to be a kind of relief to him to discuss it with Andrews, and so the latter used to humor him in it.

CHAPTER VI.

SEVERAL days after Drysdale's return from the plantation, Mrs. Potter and several others, set out for a
horseback ride. They enjoyed the afternoon exceedingly,
and it was growing dark before they reached the town on
their return. As the party passed down the street upon
which Drysdale lived, Mrs. Potter, and another lady,
lagged behind the others, and the main body were quite
a distance in advance. Mrs. Potter suggested that they
put their horses at full speed, in order to overtake their
friends. Mrs. Robbins, her companion, assented, and
they dashed off together. The latter's horse was the
faster of the two, however, and Mrs. Potter was about
fifty or sixty yards in the rear, when they approached the
Drysdale place. There was no one in sight on the
street, and there was so much foliage on each side, that
the road was quite hidden from the view of the scattered
houses.

Suddenly, Mrs. Robbins heard a shriek and a fall
behind her; quickly reining in her horse, she turned
back, passing Mrs. Potter's riderless horse on the way.
She soon discovered Mrs. Potter lying by the roadside,
groaning, and in great pain. Mrs. Robbins did not stop
to ask any questions; she saw that Mrs. Potter was badly
hurt, and she knew that assistance must be brought
instantly. She therefore, galloped up the drive to the

"She soon discovered Mrs. Potter lying by the road-side, groaning and in great pain."

Drysdale house, and hastily told them what had happened. In less than three minutes, Mr. Drysdale had improvised a stretcher out of a wicker settee and a mattress, and had summoned four stout negroes to bring it after him, while he and his wife hurried out to the road. There they found Mrs. Potter, and Mrs. Robbins supporting her. She said that she was in great pain, from severe contusion, and possible dislocation of the knee joint, and that she had also sustained some internal injuries. In a very few minutes, they had tenderly placed her on the settee, and carried her up to the house. She was carefully put to bed, and Mrs. Robbins remounted her horse to go for a physician. The latter, on his arrival, said that he could hardly tell the extent of Mrs. Potter's injuries at once, but he thought they would not confine her to her bed more than a week or two. She asked if she might be moved to the hotel, as she did not wish to trespass on Mrs. Drysdale's hospitality. Mrs. Drysdale, however, refused to hear of such a thing as the removal of a sick person from her house, and she said that she should enjoy Mrs. Potter's society enough to compensate for the slight trouble. It was decided, therefore, that Mrs. Potter should remain until she was able to go without assistance. She improved very rapidly, but her knee seemed to pain her considerably, and she spent most of her time in her room, or on a sofa under the veranda, whither her stout negro nurse used to carry her.

A few days afterwards, Mrs. Potter was lying awake in her room at about seven o'clock in the morning. Mr. and Mrs. Drysdale's room was next to hers, and the

5

transom over the connecting door was open, so that whatever was said in one room could be easily heard in the other. Mrs. Potter heard Drysdale get up and open the blinds to let in the morning sun. He had hardly done so ere he gave a sharp cry and sank into a chair.

" What is the matter ?" asked Mrs. Drysdale, in great alarm.

" Oh, nothing," he replied; " I don't feel well."

" I should think you wouldn't," said Mrs. Drysdale, " for you have had the nose-bleed terribly. Why, it is all over the pillow and floor, and leads out of the door. You must have gone down stairs."

" Yes, yes," he exclaimed, hastily, " I did get up in the night. I—I don't feel very well—I guess I will lie down again."

" Is there anything I can do for you ?" asked his wife, anxiously.

" No, nothing at present. Just go right along with your household affairs, as usual ; I shall be all right in a short time."

Mrs. Drysdale saw that her husband was nervous and irritable, and so she dressed quickly and went down to superintend her domestic duties. When Mrs. Potter's breakfast was ready, she brought it up herself and stopped a few minutes to talk.

" Do you know of any remedy for bleeding at the nose, Mrs. Potter ?" she asked. " My husband had quite a severe attack last night, and he went down on the front veranda, and then down the gravel walk, thinking, I suppose, that exercise would stop it. It must have bled frightfully, for I could see marks of blood all the way down the path to the gate."

" I suppose he let it run instead of trying to stop the flow," replied Mrs. Potter. " Some people think it is good for the health occasionally, and so they allow the nose to bleed as long as it wants to."

After a few more remarks, Mrs. Drysdale went down stairs again. Mrs. Potter could hear Mr. Drysdale tossing about on the bed in the next room, muttering to himself, and occasionally speaking aloud such expressions as— " Oh! this is horrible!"— "What does this mean?"— " My God! what could have done it?"

After a time he became quieter, but he did not leave his room until the afternoon. Soon after he got up, Mr. Andrews called to see him, having failed to find him at his office.

" I thought you might be sick and so I dropped in to see you," he said.

" I am very glad you came," replied Drysdale. " I have been a little unwell, and I need some one to cheer me up."

" Let us take a short walk," said Andrews; " the exercise will do you good."

As they strolled out, Andrews pointed to some blood and said:

" Any one hurt in your house?"

" No—yes — that is, nothing serious; one of my negroes cut his hand this morning," replied Drysdale, shuddering. " I can't look at blood without feeling sick," he explained, as he saw that Andrews was wondering at his agitation.

As they continued their walk, Andrews noticed that

Drysdale was very self-absorbed, and so they strolled down the street without conversing. Their course took them past the bank, and as Mr. McGregor was standing on the steps of the side entrance, he accosted them heartily.

"Why, how do you do, gentlemen?" he asked. "Won't you walk in for a few minutes? I havn't seen you since your illness, Mr. Drysdale; won't you come in and rest a while?"

On hearing McGregor's salutation, Drysdale started as if stung, and trembled violently. He had been walking along with his eyes down, so that he had not seen Mr. McGregor until spoken to.

"No, thank you," he replied; "I think I won't have time—that is, I promised my wife to come back soon. You must excuse me this time."

He hurried on with a nervous gesture of courtesy, and he did not recover his calmness until some minutes afterward. Andrews accompanied him to his home, and on the way they agreed to go to Drysdale's plantation for a short visit on the following Monday. Having settled upon the time for starting and returning, Andrews declined an invitation to dine with Drysdale that evening, and they separated. Andrews dropped into Breed's shop on his way back to the hotel, and there he found young Green, the man who had made his book-case. They talked together only a few minutes, and Andrews then went to his room, where he stayed the remainder of the day.

On Monday, Andrews and Drysdale rode off to the plantation at daylight, and the latter's spirits seemed to lighten rapidly after leaving the immediate vicinity of Atkinson. In the afternoon, Andrews took his gun and wandered off into the woods, but he did not seem very desirous of shooting anything, for he soon took a position whence he commanded a full view of the house. In about half an hour, Drysdale came out and walked slowly toward a small cluster of trees, about five hundred yards from the house. Here, he leaned against a tree, and paused to look around in every direction; then he began to stride with a measured step in a straight line. When he stopped, he began to examine the ground carefully for some minutes, and finally, he seemed satisfied with his inspection, and returned to the house.

During the remainder of their stay at the plantation, Andrews and Drysdale were constantly together, and the latter seemed to find the greatest pleasure in the former's society. He frequently recurred to the subject of ghosts and spooks, and always closed by discussing the character of the apparition he had seen on the roadside. There was no doubt that it had made a deep impression upon him, for he never tired of talking about it. Andrews laughed at him, ridiculed his vivid imagination, cross-questioned him, and reasoned with him upon the absurdity of his hallucination, but all to no effect; Drysdale maintained in the most dogged manner, that he had seen a ghost.

On Friday, they were to return to Atkinson, and in the morning Andrews rode over to make a short visit to a neighbor. He was so hospitably entertained, however, that he did not get away until after two o'clock, and it was nearly three before they started on their homeward ride. As before, it was growing dusky, when they reached the banks of Rocky Creek, and Drysdale was in a state of high nervous excitement.

On reaching the spot where Drysdale had seen the ghost before, he kept close at Andrews' side, and endeavored to appear unconcerned. Suddenly, he grasped Andrews by the arm with a faint groan, and said:

"Andrews, look! look! for God's sake, tell me, don't you see it?"

As he spoke, he pointed toward the same ghastly object which he had seen before. There, right under his eyes, passed the image of the murdered George Gordon.

"There, I was afraid you would have the same folly again," said Andrews, soothingly, as if anxious to attract his attention away from his ghostly friend. "What the devil is the matter with you?"

"Tell me, tell me, Andrews," gasped Drysdale, in such terror that his parched throat and quivering lips could hardly pronounce the words; "can't you see that horrible man close to the fence, walking toward the creek?"

"I tell you, my dear fellow," replied Andrews, earnestly, "that you are laboring under a most unpleasant hallucination. There is absolutely no person, or any moving object in sight, except you and me."

At this moment, the sound of approaching hoof-beats could be plainly heard, and Drysdale turned his head to look back in the direction whence they came. On looking for the ghost again, it was nowhere to be seen.

"Andrews, it is gone—the earth has swallowed it up," he said.

He would have fallen from his horse, if Andrews had

not caught him around the waist, and just as he did so, Mr. Breed and Mr. O'Fallon, the station agent, rode up, one on each side of them.

"What's the matter with Mr. Drysdale?" asked O'Fallon.

"Didn't you see it? Tell me—did the ghost pass you?" Drysdale queried eagerly, turning toward the new comers.

"What are you talking about? What do you mean by 'the ghost?'" asked Mr. Breed, in great wonderment.

"The ghost, I say—did neither of you see a horrible figure pass out of sight suddenly, toward the creek yonder?"

"I saw nothing, Mr. Drysdale," said O'Fallon; "did you, Breed?"

"Well, I don't know what Mr. Drysdale means by a ghost," said Breed, deliberately; "but I think I did see something down there. I couldn't say what it looked like. Why do you call it a ghost, Mr. Drysdale?"

"Because I have seen it twice close to me, and Mr. Andrews has not been able to see it at all," replied Drysdale with great difficulty. "I began to think it must have been imagination on my part, but now, that you have seen it, I know that it was a ghost."

Drysdale was so helpless, that it was necessary for one gentleman to ride on each side of him to hold him in his saddle. On arriving at his place, they helped him into the house, and left him in charge of his wife. He immediately went to bed, and during the night, he suffered a great deal. Mrs. Potter heard him groaning, tossing, and muttering until nearly daylight.

The story of the ghost was soon freely circulated by

O'Fallon and Breed, though they could not describe the apparition at all. Still, it created quite an excitement, and the results were not very beneficial to the neighborhood, for the reason that no negro could be induced to pass along that part of the road after dark; indeed, there were a great many educated white people who would not ride past the spot alone on a dark night.

Drysdale was confined to his room for several days, during which time he received no visitors except Andrews. It was curious to observe what a strong preference he showed for his new-found friend.

Just at this time I decided to re-visit Atkinson myself, and on my arrival there I had a long interview with Messrs. Ballantine, McGregor, and Gordon. I explained to them all the steps I had taken, and they learned to their great astonishment that Mr. Andrews, Mrs. Potter, and Mr. Green were my detectives. The ghost was Green, whose resemblance to young Gordon was a great aid in carrying out the scheme. Mrs. Potter had voluntarily fallen from her horse in order to get herself carried into Drysdale's house, and it was she who sprinkled the blood over Drysdale's clothing and down the walk. After settling all our plans, I returned to the hotel, where I was easily able to obtain a private interview with Mr. Andrews and Mr. Green.

I gave full instructions to Andrews, and he informed Mrs. Potter of my wishes, at the same time conveying to her another large bottle of blood.

CHAPTER VII.

ABOUT one o'clock that night Mrs. Potter rose, quietly dressed herself, and stealthily left the house. She walked to the nearest point on the creek and began to drop blood from her bottle. She spilled small portions of it all the way back to the house, up the front walk, in the hall, and finally, slipping into Drysdale's room, she scattered the crimson drops on his pillow. She then retired to bed.

When she awoke in the morning, she found Mrs. Drysdale in a very uneasy state of mind. She said that her husband had again been attacked by bleeding at the nose, and that he was quite weak from the loss of blood. Mrs. Potter deeply sympathized with Mrs. Drysdale, but she could assist her only by kind and consoling words.

The family had hardly finished their breakfast when a number of the neighbors came in in a high state of excitement. They said that blood had been discovered on the grass near where the ghost had been seen, and that quite a crowd had gathered around it. They had found other blood-marks at intervals along the road, and on following the direction in which they traveled, it was found that they led straight to Drysdale's house. The question now arose, did the wounded person go from the house to the creek, or *vice versa*. Drysdale was terribly excited on learning of the discovery, and he was soon in a species of delirium. It was known that he was quite sick, so that the neighbors soon withdrew. Many thought that the blood was that of a burglar or negro sneak-thief, who might have gone to Drysdale's house to steal, but who had been frightened off before he had secured any plunder. The blood might have been from an old hurt. Others, more superstitiously inclined, believed that the ghost was in some way responsible for the blood. No one was able to solve the mystery, however, and it added to the terror with which the ghost story had inspired the negroes.

Drysdale was now confined to his bed, and he would see no one except his wife and Andrews. He insisted that he was not sick, but only run down by overwork, and so refused to have a doctor. Andrews' influence over him was greater than that of any one else, and it was plain that the latter had completely secured his confidence. As I now felt convinced that Drysdale would surely confess in a short time, I returned to Chicago, leaving the whole charge of the operation with Andrews.

A few nights later Mrs. Potter was troubled with the tooth-ache, and she lay awake most of the night. Suddenly she heard footsteps in Drysdale's room, and then she saw Drysdale pass her window on the veranda. He was dressed in slippers and night-dress, and his actions were so strange that she determined to follow him. Hastily putting on some dark clothes, she hurried cautiously after him. The night was clear with no moon, and she was able to distinguish his white figure at a considerable distance. He walked rapidly to the creek and followed its windings a short distance; then he paused a few

minutes, as if reflecting. This enabled Mrs. Potter to
hide herself near by in some undergrowth, whence she
could watch him more carefully. To her great astonishment, she saw him walk into the creek at a shallow spot,
and begin wading up against the current. Very soon he
stopped and leaned over with his hands in the water, as
if he were feeling for something. In a few minutes he
came out of the stream, on the opposite side from that
on which he had entered, and took a path to a foot-
bridge leading across the creek toward his house. As
soon as she saw that he was on his way back, she hastened home as rapidly as possible, arriving there only a
few seconds before him.

The next morning, Drysdale appeared at the breakfast
table for the first time, in several days. He remarked
that he felt much better, but he said nothing of his
midnight walk, nor did his wife, as she had slept in a
separate room; however, she was probably ignorant
of it.

Neither Mrs. Potter, nor Mr. Andrews could imagine
what Drysdale's object was in making his pilgrimage to
the creek at that time of night, especially as he had
always shown the greatest aversion to that vicinity, ever
since he had first seen the ghost. I was equally puzzled
when I was informed of his freak, but I determined to
make use of the incident, in case he should do the same
thing again. I therefore instructed Andrews to have
Green watch the house every night, dressed in his apparition suit. He was then to "shadow" Drysdale, when
the latter went out, and if a favorable opportunity should

present itself, he was to appear before him in full view in the role of the ghost.

By this time, Drysdale had recovered sufficiently, to attend to his office duties, but he always seemed anxious to have Andrews with him. Andrews had talked very encouragingly to him, showing a good deal of sympathy, and thus, they had become quite confidential friends. He, therefore, assured Drysdale that he should be happy to give him as much of his company, as possible, if it would afford Drysdale any pleasure.

"You are very kind, Mr. Andrews," said Drysdale; "you may think it strange, but I feel a sense of relief, when I am with you, especially lately. I wonder if I shall ever be better," he mused plaintively.

"Why, certainly; we hope for your speedy recovery," said Andrews, cheerfully. "You let trivial matters prey on your mind, and you must stop it, for your health will not stand it."

"Well, I shall try," responded Drysdale feebly.

One evening, Mrs. Drysdale was sitting at Mrs. Potter's side, waiting for her husband's return. By this time, Mrs. Potter was able to sit up, and even to move about the room somewhat.

"My husband is failing in health, I fear," said Mrs. Drysdale.

"I am afraid so, too," replied Mrs. Potter, "and I feel sorry to think that I am a burden upon you at the same time; but, I hope to be well soon, and then I will help you take care of him."

"You have been no burden whatever, Mrs. Potter; on the contrary, your company has been a great comfort to me. But, I was thinking, that if my husband would try a change of air and life, it would be a great help to him. I should miss him sadly, but I would make any sacrifice to see him restored to health."

At the tea table, Mrs. Drysdale said:

" I was just speaking to Mrs. Potter about your health, Aleck, and I thought that if you would go away for a time, the change of scenery, and habits of life, would be very advantageous. Why don't you go down to New Orleans with Mr. Andrews? He is always talking of going there, but he is too lazy to start. You could both enjoy yourselves very much, and I know it would do you good. You would return as healthy and happy as you always used to be."

" I have been thinking of going there, or to some other place," said Drysdale, "but I can't leave just now. I think a trip would do me good, and as soon as I feel able to do so, I will get Andrews to go with me."

Nothing of interest occurred for several days. Green kept a close watch every night, but Drysdale did not appear. Andrews got Drysdale to go out hunting with him twice, but each time, Drysdale succeeded in arriving at home before dark. Green had kept up his vigils for over a week, and he began to think there was no use in them. One night, however, as he lay behind a bush, watching the house, he was suddenly aware of a white figure gliding noiselessly by him. Forewarned, though he was, the ghostly stillness with which it moved, gave him quite a severe fright, before he recollected that it was Drysdale. He immediately followed the figure and noted his every movement. In the same way, as he had done at first, he now proceeded, and after walking up the stream a short distance, he reached down, felt for something at the bottom, and then came out. As he slowly walked home, he passed within a few feet of Green, who made a considerable noise to attract his attention; but, Drysdale passed straight on, looking neither to the right nor left, and Green was unable to play ghost for the lack of an audience.

Green's account was the exact counterpart of Mrs. Potter's, and I was puzzled to account for this new move. As I sat in my office, in Chicago, with Green's report before me, the idea flashed into my mind, that possibly some of the stolen money was hidden at the bottom of the creek. Recollecting the gold pieces, which had been found on the banks of the creek, I surmised that the remainder of the gold was buried somewhere in the bed of the stream. I had no doubt of the eventual recovery of all the money, and so I decided to let that matter rest until I had complete evidence of Drysdale's guilt.

A few days after the midnight walk, Drysdale invited Andrews to make another visit to the plantation, saying,

"My overseer sends me word that he needs a great many things, and I think I had better go out to see what is wanted, myself. I would like to have you go with me, for, to tell the truth, I am almost afraid to go alone."

"I shall be very glad, indeed, to go; when shall we start?"

"Let us start Monday, and return Friday, as before," replied Drysdale.

"Very well," said Andrews. "I shall be ready on time."

At the first opportunity, Andrews informed Green of their intended visit, and told him that in order to insure the success of their plan, it would be best for him to ride out to the plantation, also, on Wednesday or Thursday. He could thus be on hand in his ghostly capacity whenever wanted. Green promised to be at a certain spot, near the plantation, on Wednesday afternoon, to receive instructions from Andrews, and all their arrangements were then completed.

Andrews took breakfast with Drysdale before starting, Monday morning, and at table, Mrs. Drysdale said:

"Aleck, Mrs. Potter is so far recovered, that I guess we shall drive out to the plantation on Wednesday or Thursday, and spend a day or two with you."

"That will be delightful," replied Drysdale, "and we shall look for you with great pleasure."

"Well, if the ladies are coming at that time, I hope they will bring our mail, for I expect an important letter," said Andrews.

"Oh, certainly," said Mrs. Drysdale; "and, if anything should prevent us from coming, I will send your letters by a servant."

Andrews had written to me of the intended visit to the plantation, and he was anxious to receive any instructions I might send, before he returned to town.

The two gentlemen mounted their horses and cantered off. Drysdale appeared in better spirits than at any time for several weeks, and by the time they reached the plantation, he was quite gay and cheerful. He had a great deal to attend to, and Andrews gave him very considerable assistance. They were kept quite constantly busy until Wednesday noon, when Mrs. Drysdale and Mrs. Potter arrived in a carriage, bringing the mail. As Andrews had expected, there was a letter for him, in which I instructed him to have Green appear to Drysdale, in the small grove of trees, where he had acted so queerly during their last visit. From Drysdale's manner in this grove, I had concluded that some of the money was buried there, and I therefore, considered it a good place for the ghost to appear.

On reading my letter, Andrews remarked that he should be obliged to go to Atkinson, to send a telegram, as his letter required an immediate answer, but that he should return the same evening. This, of course, was only an excuse to get away to meet Green, and so his horse was brought up at once, and he rode away. Green was punctual at the rendezvous, and Andrews gave him full instructions; he was to remain in sight of the house, on the side near the little grove of trees, until an opportunity should occur to appear before Drysdale. Andrews then took a long ride over the country, so as to delay his return to the plantation until after dark. During the evening, Mrs. Potter told him that Drysdale had visited the little grove that afternoon, but she was, of course, unable to follow him.

The next evening, after supper, Andrews proposed taking a short walk, and they all started out together. By chance, they took the direction of the little grove, previously mentioned, and they were all in fine spirits. Mrs. Potter, however, was obliged to walk very slowly, owing to her injured knee, and Mrs. Drysdale kept her company; the two gentlemen were, therefore, some distance in the advance, when they reached the edge of the grove. Drysdale had been unusually cheerful until then, but as they entered the shadow, he began to lose his gayety, as if something disagreeable had been suggested to him. It was now approaching twilight, and he turned toward Andrews half pettishly, and said:

"Don't go into that dismal place; let us stay out in the open walk. I never like to go into such —— "

The words died on his tongue, and he nearly fell down from fright. There, crossing their path in the sombre shades of the grove, was that terrible spectre with its ghastly face, measured step, and clotted hair. It passed into the deep recesses of the grove, while Drysdale watched it like a condemned criminal. As it moved out of sight, he fell to the ground like a dead man, and Andrews called for help. Mrs. Drysdale hurried up in great alarm, and took her husband's head in her lap, while Mrs. Potter chafed his hands and held her vinaigrette to his nostrils. Mr. Andrews quickly called some negroes from the house, and they carried their unconscious master to his room. He was soon restored to his senses, but he was in a pitiable condition. The least sound made him start like a person in the *delirium tremens*, and he muttered to himself constantly. Finally he caught Andrews by the hand and said:

"Andrews, didn't you see that horrible ghost?"

"No, indeed; I saw no ghost," replied Andrews. "Did either of you see it?" he continued, turning to the ladies.

They both answered negatively.

6

"If there really had been such a thing we certainly should have seen it," said Mrs. Potter.

"Well, I know that I saw it, and it is terrible to think that I should be the only one to whom this thing appears," said Drysdale.

Andrews handed him a drink of brandy, which revived his strength a great deal, and he again began to talk about the ghost.

"I can't understand, Andrews, why you didn't see it," he said; "it passed within fifty feet of us, and it was truly terrible."

"It is certainly very strange," replied Andrews. "Here are three persons who did *not* see it, yet you insist that you did. What did it look like? You have never yet described it to me."

Drysdale made no reply, but a look of renewed dread came over his face, and he reached for more brandy, which was given him.

"It surely must be some disease of the brain," said Mrs. Drysdale, tearfully, "for he frequently imagines that he sees strange sights, and I am afraid to think what will happen. If he would only go to some watering-place, and put himself under the care of a reliable physician, he would soon get better."

"The doctors can do me no good, my dear," he said, controlling himself by a great effort; "do not be alarmed, but let me go to sleep for a while, and I shall be better."

Mr. Andrews and Mrs. Potter left the room in a few minutes, as Mr. Drysdale evidently wished to be left alone. They had ample opportunity for consultation, and they decided that Green had better stay near by all night, to watch the house and the grove.

"If that is to be done," said Mrs. Potter, "I will go and put up a lunch which you can take to him, since if he is to remain out there all night, he will not be able to get anything to eat, and you know that a hungry ghost cannot do as well as one which is well fed."

She soon prepared a large lunch, and added to it a small bottle of wine, which she gave to Andrews. He immediately hastened out to the grove, and found Green at a point where they had agreed to meet. He gave the food to Green, and told him to keep a close watch on the house all night; in case of anything occurring he was to tap on the window of Andrews' room, which was on the ground floor. Andrews then returned to the house, leaving Green to eat his lunch, drink his wine and keep watch.

The night was damp and warm, and the insects were particularly active, so that Green's duty was none of the pleasantest. The hours slipped wearily by until after midnight, when he saw a white figure emerge from the house and approach the little grove. He hastily gained an open spot where, in the bright starlight, he could be plainly seen, and, as Drysdale advanced, he slowly paced toward him. To Green's astonishment, Drysdale passed within two feet of him without noticing his presence in any way; they passed so close to each other that Green was forced to step to one side, yet Drysdale walked slowly on until he reached the grove. Here he walked around a moment or two and then returned to the house. Green immediately tapped at Andrews' window and related what had occurred. There being no new developments, Green returned to the wood where he had picketed his horse, and then rode back to Atkinson.

CHAPTER VIII.

FRIDAY morning Drysdale appeared at breakfast and tried to appear natural and at ease. He spoke of his peculiar hallucination, but his remarks were simply repetitions of those he had frequently made before. Andrews again requested him to describe the appearance of the spectre, but Drysdale seemed averse to continuing the conversation on that subject, and so it was dropped.

Immediately after dinner they started for Atkinson, the gentlemen on horseback, and the ladies in the carriage. As Andrews could offer no plausible excuse for detaining them, Mrs. Potter was obliged to try what she could do. By making two calls on acquaintances living along the road, she was enabled to keep back their arrival much later than Drysdale liked, though not late enough for her purpose. It was too early to have Green appear, as there were so many people traveling on the road that he might be seen by others and the trick exposed.

It was quite evident that Drysdale was in a miserable condition. He was sure that he had seen the ghost of George Gordon, and he was in a state of momentary dread and suspense. He had entertained thoughts of leaving the place, but he dared not. Like Eugene Aram, he pictured himself as continually haunted by the spirit of his victim, and he feared lest others should see it, and accuse him of the murder. His health failed rapidly; his form was emaciated, his cheeks hollow, his eyes haggard and sunken. It was clearly only a question of time how soon he confessed or went insane.

Green continued his night watches about the house, and again one night Drysdale passed out to the creek and acted as before. This time, however, he had his clothes on, and as he passed Green at arms length, it seemed almost incredible that he should have failed to see him. Green took particular pains to identify the exact spot where Drysdale had searched in the water, and he marked it carefully by placing a stone on each side of the bank opposite where Drysdale had stopped.

The following night Mrs. Potter got up and went into Drysdale's room, where he was sleeping alone. She then dropped some blood on his pillow, on the floor, and around the bed. Then passing out, she left the trail as before from the house toward Rocky Creek. Drysdale was horrified early next morning when he saw the blood-stains. He groaned piteously as he walked about the room, and then followed the spots out to the front gate. On seeing that they continued beyond this, he came back with a most dejected and helpless look. Mrs. Potter saw him go into his room, and, by looking through the key-hole of the connecting door, she was enabled to see that he was engaged in washing out the spots on the floor and bed clothes. He did not appear at the breakfast table, but his wife told Mrs. Potter that he had had another severe attack of bleeding during the night, and that he was very weak in consequence.

During the forenoon Mrs. Potter went in to see Mr.

Drysdale, whom she found in great distress physically and mentally. He was anxious to see Mr. Andrews, and his wife sent a message to the hotel at once. In about an hour Andrews came in.

"I am sorry to find you feeling so bad this morning," he said. "You were looking quite well last evening. What is the trouble? Wouldn't you like me to go for a doctor?"

"No, thank you; I shall get along better without physic," replied Drysdale. "I was feeling unusually well last evening, but I had a severe attack of bleeding last night, and I am very weak."

"Is there anything I can do for you?" asked Andrews.

"Well, yes; there are some papers in my office that should be sent to Captain Rowland, a planter in the west end of the county, and as it is important that they should be delivered soon, I should be greatly obliged if you would get them and send them off."

"Certainly, certainly," said Andrews; "where shall I find them?"

"They are in the left-hand pigeon-hole of my upright desk, in the office, and you can send them by Dan. Marston, who lives near the court-house; he is very faithful and trustworthy. Any one can tell you where to find him."

"Oh, I know Dan.," said Andrews, "he has done several errands for me. Where are your keys?"

"They are on the bureau, yonder; but, Andrews, I wish you would come back after you have sent the papers. I always feel better when I hear you talking;

when I am alone I keep thinking about that spirit, and I tell you it is terrible. You will come back, won't you?"

"Oh, certainly; I shall be glad to keep you company while you are under the weather."

When Andrews started off with the keys, a sudden thought flashed into his mind, and he first went to his room, where he obtained some blood, of which he had quite a supply. He then went to Drysdale's private office and dropped some blood on the desk, chairs and floor, and also on the wrapper of Captain Rowland's papers. He was well known to the deputy clerk, and so no one questioned his right to go to Drysdale's desk. On leaving the private office, he locked the door, and hurried back to Drysdale's house with the papers. He entered Drysdale's room in an excited manner, and said:

"Why, Drysdale, you must have been bleeding at the office, for there is blood on your chairs, desk, and on these papers; look there!"

As he spoke, he held out the package with its dull, crimson stain. The shock was too much for Drysdale, and he fainted away instantly. It was sometime before he revived, but finally, he was able to talk again.

"Please take the wrapper off those papers," he said feebly, "and put them into another. They are copies of papers in a law case now in court, and I would not like them to go out in that condition."

Andrews agreed to fix them all neat and clean before sending them, and he then went out to attend to it. On his way down town, he met Mr. McGregor, to whom he related what he had done, and its effect.

"Mr. McGregor," he continued, "I think it would be

a good idea to sprinkle some blood in the bank, on the floor, and on the desk, where young Gordon used to stand; also, to put some blood and hair on the canceling hammer. Do this in the evening, and arrange to have some one enter the bank with you in the morning; then, the story will be circulated until Drysdale will hear it, and it may have a powerful effect upon him. I think Mr. Pinkerton would approve the plan, if he were here."

Mr. McGregor thought favorably of the suggestion, and he agreed to act upon it, as soon as possible. Andrews then went back to Drysdale's office, wiped up the blood spots, and put Captain Rowland's papers into a new wrapper. Having sent them off, he returned and passed the afternoon with Drysdale.

The latter was in a terrible condition; he seemed like a man suffering from hydrophobia, so sensitive were his nerves, and so depressed was his mind. His thoughts could turn in only one direction, and that was toward remorse and fear.

> "'Tis guilt alone,
> Like brain sick frenzy in its feverish mood,
> Fills the light air with visionary terrors
> And shapeless forms of fear."

Through advices from Andrews, I was aware that things were approaching a crisis, and I therefore, went immediately to Atkinson, in order to be ready for any emergency. I arrived there the very morning chosen by Mr. McGregor, to carry out his project of sprinkling blood at the bank. He had arranged, by apparent accident, to have two planters enter the bank with him, and in fact, it happened that four gentlemen were present at ten o'clock when he opened the bank. They all entered together, and when Mr. McGregor had taken down the blinds, he went inside the bank railing. As he did so, he uttered a sudden exclamation, which caused the others to follow.

"What can this mean!" he said, in an excited tone.

The other gentlemen gathered around the ghastly scene and examined the blood, which lay in a pool on the floor, and in spots on the furniture and wall. The canceling hammer, stained with blood, and clotted with hair, lay close by, and every one was reminded of the appearance of the place, the morning after George Gordon's murder.

"What can have happened?" asked old Mr. Gordon, who had just entered. "Surely, no one was murdered here last night."

"Ah! I fear it is done by poor George's spirit!" exclaimed O'Fallon, who was a very superstitious man. "This looks just as it did that fatal morning, except that the body is not here. His spirit must be uneasy at the failure to discover his murderer."

By this time, Flanders and several others, had entered the bank, and the appearance of things there, was soon circulated throughout the town. The excitement about the murder, was revived in all its original importance, and many were the speculations about the mysterious affair.

Drysdale felt rather strong that morning, and about noon, he walked down to his gate. While there, some of his neighbors passed on their way to their homes, and they were all anxious to tell him about the new sensation at the bank. On hearing the news, Drysdale dragged himself into the house and went to bed. There he lay, groaning and sobbing piteously, and when Andrews called in the afternoon, he was so helpless that Andrews insisted on calling a physician. In a short time he returned with Dr. Sprague, who examined the patient, and prescribed for him. Dr. Sprague said that Drysdale would speedily recover with a proper amount of rest and sleep. Wakefulness and nervous irritation seemed to be the trouble with him, and the doctor told Andrews that he had prescribed morphine. He said that there was nothing serious to fear unless fever should set in, and if any symptoms should show themselves it would be necessary to call him immediately.

Upon leaving Drysdale, Andrews came to me to report. I had arranged with Mr. McGregor, to pay a visit to the creek that night, to search the spot which had been visited so often by Drysdale. I therefore sent Andrews back to offer to remain with Drysdale during the night. This arrangement pleased Drysdale very much, and he was quite touched by Andrews kindness. I also instructed Green to watch Drysdale's house, so as to be ready to appear before Drysdale, in case the latter left his house. He was to cross and re-cross Drysdale's path, until Drysdale should take notice of him, while Andrews was to be at hand immediately, pretending that he had fallen asleep during his watch, and on waking up suddenly and finding Drysdale gone, had come out in search of him.

I told Mr. Bannatine and Mr. McGregor, to bring a wheelbarrow, pick-axe, and large shovel with them, since we should probably need the two latter to dig up the gold, while the wheelbarrow would be handy to carry it home. Everything was provided for in advance, and I felt confident of the success of our expedition.

"He was forced to visit the spot where his blood-stained treasure was concealed, even in his hours of repose."

CHAPTER IX.

THE night was clear and bright, and everything was favorable for our work. At twelve o'clock, we met as previously agreed, and hastened to the banks of Rocky Creek, at the spot which Green had pointed out to me that day. On reaching the designated place, I threw off my coat and waded into the creek. I soon found a large flat stone, which I removed to one side. I was just beginning to dig under it, when Green hurried up and told me that Drysdale had left the house, and that he was only a short distance behind. We quickly hid ourselves in the underbrush, and in a few moments Drysdale appeared. Green passed him back and forth, several times, but Drysdale paid no attention to him whatever. Suddenly the thought flashed upon me, that he was walking in his sleep, and I soon saw that such was the case. All of his midnight promenades were now accounted for, and it was not strange that he had not noticed Green. So great was the man's anxiety and nervous dread of discovery, that he could not rest in quiet, and he was forced to visit the spot where his blood-stained treasure was concealed, even in his hours of repose.

He now waded into the creek, as before, but he remained a much longer time than usual, as he was unable to find the large flat stone in its accustomed spot. Finally, he discovered where I had thrown it, and he immediately replaced it in the very hole whence I had taken it. He then returned to the house, and went to bed.

I again removed the stone, and while Mr. McGregor handled the pick-axe, I plied the shovel vigorously. In a very few minutes, we struck a piece of wood which gave back a hollow sound. This encouraged us to renewed activity, and we were richly rewarded by un-earthing a large cheese-box, whose weight gave ample proof of the value of its contents. Having replaced the flat stone where we first found it, we put the box on the wheelbarrow, and took turns in wheeling it to the bank, where we soon broke it open and discovered, as we had expected, that it was full of gold coin in rouleaux. The counting of this large sum of money was rather tedious, but it was finally accomplished satisfactorily, and the result showed that only eighty dollars were missing.

The officers of the bank were in high glee, and they asked me whether I had any hope of recovering the paper money.

"If I am not mistaken," I replied, "I shall find the paper money also, within twenty-four hours. I shall go to Drysdale's plantation to-morrow night, and shall search the ground in that group of trees of which you have already heard so much. I think we shall find there all the paper money."

The next day, Drysdale and Andrews remained together constantly; indeed, Drysdale did not seem willing to let Andrews leave his sight for a moment. He was perfectly helpless and inert. In the evening, I met my companions of the night previous, and we drove out to Drysdale's plantation, taking along the necessary tools. We secured our horses in the grove, and then Green led the way toward the spot where Drysdale had examined the ground. On making a close examination with our dark lanterns, we discovered a piece of sod which had evidently been taken up, for the edges had not yet joined with the surrounding turf. We quickly pulled it up and began to dig beneath it; as before, our search was rewarded after a few minutes of labor. At the depth of two feet, we came upon a large candle-box, which we carefully dug up and placed in one of our buggies. There was apparently, nothing more concealed in this spot, and so we replaced the earth, packed it down, and put the piece of sod back into its place. We then returned to Atkinson, where we arrived just before daylight. The bank officers immediately opened the box, and counted the paper money contained therein; it was found to agree exactly, with the sum stolen from the bank. The packages of bills were replaced in the box, which was then locked up in the vault.

I sent instructions by Andrews to Mrs. Potter to again make use of the blood about Drysdale's house, and I also ordered Green to keep watch during the night. The next morning Andrews reported that Drysdale's terror on discovering the blood had been greater than he had ever shown before, and that he was fast breaking down. I therefore held a consultation with the bank officers.

"Now, gentlemen," I said, "we have recovered the money, and we have sufficient evidence to convict the murderer. I think it is time to arrest him; don't you?"

To tell the truth, I was in no easy frame of mind myself. I was morally sure of Drysdale's guilt, but I had no legal evidence which was sufficient to convict him in case he should maintain his innocence. Moreover I had assumed a terrible responsibility in taking such extreme measures with him, for there was danger that he might go insane without confessing his guilt, and in that case my position would have been really dangerous. I should have been accused of driving him crazy with no proper justification for my actions, and the result might have been most disastrous to me. The fact that I, an unknown man from the North, had driven a high-toned Southern gentleman insane, would have been sufficient to hang me by the summary process of lynch law.

The fact that part of the money had been found on his plantation, would be only circumstantial evidence, since another man might have buried it there as well as Drysdale. His visits to the spots where the money was concealed, were not conclusive of guilt, since he was a somnambulist, and in his sleep-walking he was not responsible for his actions. Mrs. Potter suggested to me that he might have been sleep-walking the night of the murder, and (while in that condition,) he might have followed the murderer to the spot where the gold was hidden; it would then be nothing strange that he should go to the same spot in his subsequent night-wanderings.

It will thus be easily understood that during the remainder of my connection with the case, I was in a highly wrought up frame of mind. Indeed, when I came to make the arrest, it would have been hard to tell whether Drysdale or I was the more excited. In reply to

my question, Mr. Bannatine instructed me to take whatever course I saw fit, as they were all perfectly satisfied
with my management of the affair. I learned from
Andrews that Drysdale would visit his office that afternoon, as there were some important matters requiring
his attention. Drysdale had told Andrews that he
intended to put the office in the charge of a deputy for a
time, so as to enable him to go off to New Orleans on a
visit of several weeks, and he desired that Andrews should
accompany him. He little thought that the toils were
closing around him so rapidly, and that he should never
start on his projected excursion.

Having decided to arrest him immediately, I went to
the office of an old friend of Mr. Bannatine, a lawyer,
who drew up the necessary affidavit upon which I proposed to apply for a warrant. I then called upon the
sheriff, and asked him to go before a justice of the peace
with me, while I swore to an affidavit for a warrant which
I wished him to execute.

"What is the warrant for?" asked the sheriff, as he
walked along with me.

"It is quite an important case," I replied, "and I have
had the affidavits drawn up by Mr. Wood, the lawyer, and
you will see the charge in a few minutes."

"All right," said the sheriff; "let us go to Squire
Baker's."

Fortunately we found the justice alone, and having
stated that I wished to obtain a warrant, I handed him
the affidavit which I had had prepared. He carefully
adjusted his glasses and began to read the paper, but in
a moment or two he gave a sudden start and dropped the

document, in utter amazement. He looked at me keenly and said :

"Do you mean to accuse Mr. Drysdale of murdering George Gordon?"

At this the sheriff was equally astonished, and he said :

"Oh! nonsense; it can't be possible. Why, do you know, my dear sir, that he is one of the finest gentlemen, and one of the most honorable men in Atkinson? Surely you are joking."

"No, I am not joking at all," I replied. "I knew, of course, that you would be greatly surprised and shocked, but the proofs are too clear to admit of any doubt. The matter has been carefully examined by Mr. Bannatine, Mr. Gordon, and Mr. McGregor, and it is at their request that I have come to get a warrant. However, I can soon convince you of his guilt."

"Well, well, it is almost incredible," said Squire Baker, "but if Mr. Bannatine and Mr. McGregor are convinced, I presume there must be strong grounds for suspicion, for they are both very careful men. I certainly hope, however, that it may prove to have been a mistake, and that Mr. Drysdale will be able to show his innocence."

I then made oath to the facts, and the warrant was issued. The sheriff asked me when he should make the arrest, and I told him that Drysdale was then at his office, and he must be taken at once. We accordingly, went straight to his office, where we found him with Andrews. As the sheriff entered, Drysdale said :

"How do you do, Mr. Ringwood? Take a chair."

"No, I thank you, Mr. Drysdale," said the sheriff in a sympathetic tone; "the fact is, I am here on a very unpleasant duty, and I cannot stay long. I have a warrant for your arrest, Mr. Drysdale."

"Warrant for me! what for?" exclaimed Drysdale, huskily.

"It is for the murder of George Gordon," replied the sheriff.

"Who charges me? I——"

Drysdale could only shriek the above, ere he fell back into a chair almost lifeless. In a few minutes, he recovered somewhat, and the sheriff said:

"Mr. Pinkerton here, has made an affidavit to the charge, and he seems to be acquainted with the grounds for accusing you; suppose you walk down to the bank with us."

Drysdale gazed at me steadily for a moment, and then said:

"Let me look at the warrant."

He was trembling like an aspen leaf, while he was reading it, and when he had finished, he expressed a willingness to go with us, if Andrews would go too. It was now after banking hours, and the bank was closed, but the officers admitted us. After the door had been closed, I turned to Drysdale and said:

"I have the unpleasant duty, Mr. Drysdale, of charging you with the murder of George Gordon, in this bank; have you any denial to make?"

This was the signal to Green, and as I finished speaking, he passed from behind the desk, where he had been seated, across the spot where Gordon's body had fallen. He was made up exactly like Gordon, as on previous occasions, and though he was in sight only a second, it

7

was enough. Drysdale gave a shriek, and fell lifeless, as the apparent ghost disappeared in the vault. It was done so quickly, that even the sheriff was puzzled to determine what the apparition was. Restoratives were applied, and Drysdale soon revived.

"Great God!" he exclaimed. "Where is George Gordon? I am sure he was here. Did you see him, Andrews?"

No one answered, and seeing that we were all looking at him in amazement, he sprang to his feet, exclaiming:

"I deny the charge you have made against me; it is false in every particular."

"Then, Mr. Drysdale," said I, "you will probably deny that you buried the gold, which was taken from this bank, in the bed of Rocky Creek. Here it is," I added, uncovering the box, which had been placed near by.

He said nothing, but hung his head, and drew a long breath.

"Will you also deny that you buried the paper money in a grove near your house, on your plantation?" I continued, showing him the candle box.

He still said nothing, and I made a motion to Andrews to have Green ready for a re-appearance. Then I went on speaking.

"This money has all been identified as that which was stolen from the bank; it was found as I have stated. I also have here a partly burned note of yours, which you used to light the fire in the grate. I have examined these fragments of buttons, and I find that they are exactly like those on the coat which you brought home from New

"Drysdale gave a shriek, and fell lifeless, as the apparent ghost disappeared in the vault."

Orleans just before the murder; they were found in the grate yonder, where you burned your coat, but there is enough left of them to identify them. But if you are not satisfied with this evidence, that we can prove you are guilty, I will even call upon the murdered man himself, to testify against you."

As I spoke, Green slowly glided out toward us, with his white, set face, and bloody hair. Drysdale covered his face with his hands, dropped into a chair and shrieked :

"Oh! my God! I am guilty! I am guilty!" and he sank back, but did not faint.

Green instantly retired, whence he came, and Drysdale continued speaking, as if he obtained relief by confessing his crime.

"Yes, I am guilty, and I have suffered the tortures of the damned since that frightful night. I do not know what made me do it, but I have never known a moment's peace since then. My mind has been occupied with that money constantly, and even in my sleep I would dream about it. Oh! it is terrible!"

"Have you ever gone to look for it at night, Mr. Drysdale ?" I asked, as I wished to know whether he was aware of his somnambulism.

"Oh, no; I would not dare to go near it, but it has haunted me always."

"How did you come to murder George?" I asked.

"I can't tell," he replied, in a choking voice; "it all occurred like a dream."

"What motive did you have ? You surely could have

got money without resorting to robbery, much less murder."

"No, I could not. People think I am wealthy, but the fact is I lost a great deal of money in speculating when I went to New Orleans, a few months before the murder, and although I have a good deal of property, I had no ready money, and I could not work my plantation properly for want of it. I had purchased seven slaves from a man in New Orleans, and I could not pay for them. He was pressing me for the money, about twelve hundred dollars, and I came down to the bank to get the money from George. I had only three hundred dollars in bank, and so I gave my note for the remainder. While George was counting out the money, I was taken with a sort of insanity, and I struck him with a large hammer which happened to be at hand. Then I carried off the money and buried it, since which time I have never touched it. It has been a curse to me. This is all I have to say now."

I turned to Mr. Bannatine and said:

"I have now done all that I can do in this matter, I think."

"Yes, you have completed your task, and the law must now take its course," he replied. "Mr. Ringwood, you had better take charge of Mr. Drysdale."

Drysdale rose from his chair, wearily, and said:

"I am glad the end has come at last. This affair has been killing me by inches, and I am glad I have confessed."

The sheriff then touched him on the shoulder and said that he must go.

"Yes, I am ready," he replied, "but please let me speak a few words privately, to Mr. Andrews; I want to send a message to my wife," he added, with a sob.

He and Andrews then stepped into the small private office, and Andrews closed the door behind him.

"Andrews, my friend," said Drysdale, convulsively, "I beg you to break this news to my poor wife. God help her and the children. Tell her that I feel better for having confessed, and whatever happens she must keep up her courage. Now, my dear friend, good bye. Tell the sheriff to come here and take me to jail."

He wrung Andrews' hand warmly as the latter stepped to the door, but before the latter had reached us, we heard the ringing report of a pistol shot. We made a simultaneous rush for the little room, but we were too late. There, quivering on the floor, with a bullet in his brain, lay the murderer of George Gordon. The crime and the avengement had occurred in the same building, only a few feet separating the spot where the two bodies had fallen. The somnambulist had walked on earth for the last time.

THE END.

ALSO AVAILABLE

Captain J. N. Sumner from Springfield, Massachusetts, hires Pinkerton to help solve a crime involving his sisters and the deed to a family farm. His younger sister Annie falls under the charms of a married man, Mr. Pattmore, who promises to marry Annie once his wife and her brother are out of the way. Captain Sumner possesses an opal ring with a stone that appears to foretell events. After suddenly falling violently ill, he becomes convinced his sister is trying to poison him to get his fortune and, more importantly, his ring.

Recognizing Annie's superstitious nature, Pinkerton has one of his female detectives pose as a fortune-teller to meet with Annie. But it soon becomes clear that Pinkerton may have gotten more than he bargained for. Is Annie actually trying to kill her brother, or is she being controlled by a much more sinister force? Is Captain Sumner's ring genuine? So unfolds this tale of adultery, politics, superstition, manipulation, and murder. Paper $15.95, ISBN 978-1-60635-416-2

This collaboration with Kent State University Special Collections and Archives brings these classic books from the Borowitz Collection back in print.

"The Borowitz Collection is the greatest private true crime library ever amassed."—Laura James, attorney and true crime writer, author of *The Beauty Defense: Femmes Fatales on Trial*

BLACK SQUIRREL BOOKS®

an imprint of The Kent State University Press
www.KentStateUniversityPress.com